The Ranger Takes a Bride

Texas Rancher Trilogy

Book 2

Misty M. Beller

This book is a work of fiction and any resemblance to persons, living or dead, or places, events or locales is purely coincidental. The characters are the product of the author's imagination and used fictitiously.

ISBN: 0-9982087-2-8
ISBN-13: 978-0-9982087-2-5

Dedication

To my husband.
For his commitment and caring,
and the many little ways he shows them both.
I'm thankful God brought us together.

The Lord is my light and my salvation;
Whom shall I fear?
The Lord is the strength of my life;
Of whom shall I be afraid?

Psalms 27:1 (KJV)

Chapter One

November 20, 1875

Rancho Las Cuevas, Tamaulipas, Mexico

ALEJANDRA Diaz picked her way across the rocky ground, a band of dread tightening her chest. This was not a message she wanted to give, but desperation compelled her.

Reaching the rough wooden door of the adobe hut, she rapped lightly with one hand and pushed it ajar with her other. "Mama Sarita?"

"Sí, mija."

As Alejandra's eyes adjusted to the dim light of the room, she focused on the slender figure standing by the work table. Mama Sarita held knife in hand, poised over something on the counter. Red peppers most likely, judging by the sweet aroma lacing the air. But the woman's eyes focused on Alejandra, and the love that usually shone there mixed with wariness and fear.

Forcing her feet to carry her forward, Alejandra blinked back tears as she stood in front of the woman who had become as dear to her as her own sweet mama had been. But Mama Sarita wasn't her mother. She was Luis' mama. The *madre* of her *prometido*—promised one. And now he was gone, and it was up to Alejandra to break the news.

"Mama Sarita." Alejandra stopped to force moisture into her parched throat.

"What is it, child?" Mama Sarita raised a hand to cup Alejandra's cheek. The calluses on the woman's work-roughened fingers were the touch of love.

Alejandra's eyes and throat burned with the sting of tears. "Mama. The news is bad, *es terrible*."

Mama Sarita's palm dropped from Alejandra's cheek to clutch her hand. "My Luis? And Ricardo?" Her grip tightened on Alejandra's palm, but it was a welcome pain.

"I'm so sorry, Mama." Alejandra couldn't hold back the tears anymore, as they streamed down her face. "The soldiers killed them both. And my papa, too. Señor Salinas and eighty men. All gone at the hands of the...American Rangers." Alejandra spat out the last words, almost choking on them.

Mama Sarita pulled her into a tight embrace. The feel of this madre's arms was more than Alejandra could resist, and she allowed the sobs to overcome her body. First her own mother had been murdered at the hands of French soldiers all those years ago. Now Papa. And Luis, her promised one and best hope for a suitable husband. And Papa Ricardo, Luis' padre.

A wave of realization washed over Alejandra. Now she and Mama Sarita had only each other. In one fell swoop, the soldiers had left them both alone and abandoned.

Alejandra clutched the woman's swaying body tighter. As long as there was breath in her body, Mama Sarita would never be alone.

ALEJANDRA ladled the atole into a bowl, then settled a spoon into the thick, grainy liquid. Mama Sarita liked atole with plenty of ground corn so it was more like a porridge than a drink, so that's exactly how Alejandra made it. Mama Sarita said it kept her menfolk full longer, so they could work harder. She always patted Papa Ricardo's muscular shoulder when she said the words. The love between them always lit the small adobe dwelling. Pain seared Alejandra's heart at the memory—partly because she mourned the loss of the three men who had meant the most to her, and partly because of the agony Mama Sarita must be experiencing. Papa Ricardo and Luis had been her world.

Swallowing back fresh tears, she carried the bowl to the front doorway and sat next to the hunched figure seated on the stoop. "I brought your breakfast. Thick, warm atole."

Mama Sarita accepted the bowl Alejandra placed in her hands, but her eyes stared out across the narrow dusty road that ran in front of the hut. The trail passed by each of the ranch worker huts nestled in openings in the trees, and eventually ended at the Rincon de Cucharras outpost of the vast Rancho Las Cuevas.

Rancho Las Cuevas had been her and Papa's home for these six years, but much longer for Mama Sarita. How long had Luis said? They'd come here when he was but a child of five. And now, he would have celebrated his veinte años in less than a week. Twenty years. Except the American soldiers killed him. Alejandra fought the urge to hit something. But instead, she raised her hand to finger the scar that marred her right cheek, extending from her cheekbone to the base of her ear. Yes, soldiers brought nothing but pain and heartache.

"What was the fighting about, mija?" Mama Sarita's voice drifted through the tirade in Alejandra's mind.

She turned to look at the older woman. But Mama Sarita still stared into the distance, over the road and into the woods beyond.

Alejandra swallowed. "I'm not sure exactly. There was trouble with some cattle. I think our *vaqueros* brought the animals across the Rio Bravo, and the *soldados Americano* wanted to take them back. They killed Señor Salinas and eighty of our vaqueros."

"So the cattle belonged to the Americanos?"

Alejandra jerked her attention to Mama Sarita's face. The leathery skin between her brows pinched, as if she were trying to decipher a mystery.

"Sí, mama."

4

"And they took the animals back across the river?"

"Sí." What was Mama Sarita trying to determine? If the Americanos were in the right? Of course not. They were soldiers, invading a land that wasn't their own and murdering innocent people. Murdering Papa.

The thrumming of hoof beats in the distance finally brought Mama Sarita's head around. Through the trees, a rider became visible. A man wearing the wide-brimmed hat of a vaquero. As he reined his bay to a stop in front of them, a cloud of dust rose into the dry air. He removed his hat to swipe the dust away, exposing unruly black hair and thick brows, a perfect match to his long mustache.

Alejandra rose to her feet in deference to Señor Vegas, one of the foremen at the outpost. Mama Sarita didn't leave her perch on the step.

"Buenos dias, Señora Garza. Señorita Diaz. I'm glad to find you together." He nodded to them both, his mustache curving down as his mouth pinched.

"Señor Vegas." Mama Sarita's greeting held a quiet authority.

"My news is not good. You know of the fighting with the Texas Rangers, si?"

Alejandra nodded.

"Many vaqueros were lost. Your men among them." He paused and eyed them both, as if assessing whether they'd heard the news already.

The now-familiar burn pricked Alejandra's throat and stung her eyes. But through her blurry vision, she glimpsed a nod from Mama Sarita. Did the older woman not have any tears left? Or was she still in shock, not fully understanding what had happened?

The man continued. "As you know, the houses you both live in are ranch property. For the vaqueros and their families." His fingers squeezed the round crown of his hat, crunching it like soft cotton. "Since you don't have men to work on the ranch...." he stopped to clear his throat, "you must plan to leave."

He looked down, apparently lacking courage to meet their expressions. And that may have been a wise choice, but Alejandra still did her best to burn a hole through him with her gaze. How dare this man throw them out of their homes?

A motion in the corner of Alejandra's gaze caught her attention, and she turned to watch Mama Sarita slowly unfold herself from the stoop and rise. An Aztecan queen never moved with such regal bearing, such quiet nobility. She stepped forward, stopping a length away from Señor Vegas.

"Señor." Mama Sarita's voice was strong. "I would like to inquire after work—at the main house or one of the outposts. I am willing to clean or cook for the Don and Doña. Alejandra would make an excellent nurse for the wee babe."

The man shook his head before she was half through with her request. He held up a hand to silence any further words. "Señora. So many vaqueros have left wives. There is not work enough in all Tamaulipas for them to be cooks and housekeepers. You must go."

6

With those final words, he jerked the horse's reins to spin the animal around. The unsuspecting gelding threw up its nose, eyes wide, before it acceded to the pull and spun toward the road.

Señor Vegas reined in the animal after only a few strides, then turned in the saddle to look back at them. "Señora, it will be a few days before the new vaqueros arrive. You may have until Saturday to move your belongings."

Three days. They had three days to close out the remnants of life as they knew it and create a new purpose.

As the anger that had coursed through Alejandra's veins dissipated, despair filled its place, pushing down on her shoulders like layers of thick woolen ponchos.

Mama Sarita turned, still standing near the road where she'd spoken to the foreman. Her face mirrored the same weariness that pressed down on Alejandra's spirit. Mama Sarita wasn't an old woman—barely past child-bearing years. But the deep lines that formed around her mouth, eyes, and forehead gave the appearance she had lived more than one lifetime.

And maybe she had. After all, hadn't she grown up in *América*? Living in another world, until Papa Ricardo won her heart and brought her to live in Mexico. *Como México no hay dos,* Papa Ricardo always said. Mexico is second to none. After living so many years in this land, Mama Sarita almost looked like a native now, despite her dark brown hair and rich cocoa eyes. Her skin had leathered under the Southern sun, and she spoke the language like any countryman. Yes, Mama Sarita belonged here.

A surge of love welled in Alejandra's chest, and she stepped forward to take Mama Sarita's arm. "Come, Mama. Eat, and then we will make plans."

NOVEMBER 21, 1875
SAN ANTONIO, TEXAS

EDWARD Stewart gave the outlaw a shove as the man shuffled into the small jail cell. Neither of them spoke while he swung the metal door shut and turned the key. A click radiated through the small room, and he gave the door a sound shake to make sure it was secure. The man inside grunted as he plopped into an old spindle-back chair, then folded his greasy head into his hands.

Edward spun on his heel and strode out of the jail area, into the front office. They'd been traveling most of the day without stopping for food or drink, so the prisoner would need rations. He couldn't bring himself to hurry, though. It was hard to pity a man who would steal from innocent women and children.

As he tossed the jail key on the deputy's desk, a rush of adrenaline blasted through him. Another assignment complete. Another scoundrel behind bars. The Texas Rangers were victorious again.

He met the deputy's gaze with a nod. "He's locked up and still cuffed. Might get a bit hungry soon, but I'm not worried about 'im."

The deputy stroked his mustache. "We'll keep him secure 'til the judge comes around. Just leave yer report."

Edward turned, lifted his hat, and scraped a hand through his hair. "I'm a bit short on grub. I'll write out the details while I eat a bite at the Riverwalk."

He strode out the front door and through the gate that surrounded the jail and courthouse, then fell into stride on the road with the other passersby and wagons. A sea of people going every direction. And where was he headed? Where did this vacant spot in his chest tell him to go?

For two years now, he'd been a Texas Ranger. Part of the family of men who'd built a reputation as tough lawmen, the bravest in any territory. And among the Rangers, he worked hard to be one of the best. A far cry from "Little Brother," as the cowpunchers called him when he'd worked on his sister's ranch back home. So why wasn't it enough?

Edward stepped up on the boardwalk, then veered around a well-dressed couple strolling down the center of the wood plank walkway. The woman wore gobs of lace and finery, and her laughter tinkled like a bell on the breeze.

Maybe he needed a woman. A pretty little flower to walk on his arm and laugh at his jokes. But when exactly would he have time to escort a wife around town? Ranger assignments kept him traveling for days at a time, with a short night or two at home before he climbed back in the saddle for the next job.

9

Nope. There was good reason why most Rangers remained unmarried.

So what is it, Lord? What am I missing?

The question reverberated in Edward's chest as he pushed through the swinging doors of the Riverwalk Café. There'd be time to dwell on that empty feeling later. Now was his chance for a decent meal, before he had to saddle his horse and track down another desperado.

Chapter Two

ALEJANDRA scanned the bare edges of the room that had been her home these eight years. Memories of Papa filled the space. His favorite chair at the table. Even the stove with its rusty door that often lifted off the hinges. None of the other vaquero huts had a stove like this. But Papa had appeared outside one day, driving a ranch wagon with the big, iron contraption in the back. How hard had he worked and bartered to obtain such a luxury for her? By the time he had it set up, his leathery wrinkles had been covered in black soot. If she closed her eyes, she could still see the sparkle in his eyes as he watched her cook at the stove that first time. Wrapping her arms around her middle, Alejandra could almost snuggle into his warm hug and hear him call her *Mija* again. My little girl.

"Papa." The word drifted from her, but Alejandra fought to hold the tears inside.

A mew answered her from the corner, and a little bundle of fur scampered to Alejandra's feet. The kitten let loose a string of cries as it sat at the base of her brown skirt and raised a paw to tap the fabric.

Alejandra reached down to scoop up the pesky gray fur ball. "Rudy."

Ruidoso rubbed his head under her chin and meowed again, even as his chest picked up a steady satisfied rumble.

"You're a pesky little kitten." But Alejandra obliged him and scratched the bony joints under each of his ears. Funny how an animal could always lift her spirits.

"Come on, fellow. We have to get our things to Mama Sarita's. She needs us." The squirmy cat responded with another cry.

A rap on the door grabbed Alejandra's attention. It was too soft to be one of the vaqueros. Mama Sarita?

But when she cracked the door, a younger face smiled back at her.

"Buenos dias, Alejandra." Elena Gomez stood on the stoop, her baby girl smiling out of the sling across her chest.

"Elena." Alejandra opened the door wider and stepped back. "And little Damaris. Please, come in."

Elena hesitated. "I just came to check on you. I'm making rounds to all the women who lost their men in the *batalla*."

Alejandra spun on her heel and strode further into the room. "I was just leaving. I'm going to stay with Mama Sarita until we decide where to go." The woman surely meant well, but it galled her to think Elena Gomez or anyone else pitied her. Alejandra had always been able to hold her head high. Now was no different.

Scooping up the two bundles she'd packed, she plopped one into Elena's arms and tucked the other under her elbow. "You can help me carry these." With her free hand, Alejandra grabbed Papa's rifle from the pegs on the wall, then stalked out the door. "Come on, Rudy."

"Have you already taken the rest of your things?" Elena huffed as she struggled to catch up with Alejandra. The sun cast warm rays, even though the calendar said winter should be upon them soon.

Remorse pricked her chest, and Alejandra slowed to allow the other woman to keep pace. But she ignored the question. Elena didn't need to know her only possessions were a spare dress, two blankets, a few food scraps, Mama's Bible, and Papa's gun. And Rudy. If at all possible, she would take the bothersome cat wherever she and Mama Sarita went.

"Do you know where you'll go?" Elena's child whined from the sling, probably because of the jarring pace. The young mother spoke soothing words to her babe, and Alejandra slowed her steps even more. Elena didn't mean to be annoying with her questions.

When the baby stopped fussing, Elena looked at Alejandra, but kept her steady pace. "So do you know where you'll go?"

Alejandra raised a shoulder in a casual movement. Apparently the woman wouldn't be put off. "Not sure."

"I've heard there are lots of jobs in Nuevo Laredo, even for women. Hotels in need of cleaning maids and cooks. Sewing rooms that make fabric and clothing and blankets. So many options."

Elena seemed so proud of her news. And it was kind of her to share. But working in a small dark room hunched over a needle or loom didn't sound like a fiesta. And cleaning up after strangers? Alejandra swallowed a lump in her throat. Cooking didn't sound so bad, though. Maybe she and Mama Sarita could work together in the same kitchen. Would God be so kind as to allow them that one small mercy? Did He even care? Not if *she* asked, but maybe He would listen if Mama Sarita made the request.

They'd finally reached the older woman's door, and Alejandra tapped her knuckle. "Mama Sarita?"

"Come in, mija."

Alejandra pushed the door open and stuck her head in. Mama sat on the edge of the bed in the corner, a stack of papers in her hand. Her face creased into a smile aimed straight at Alejandra. A weight lifted in Alejandra's chest, and she couldn't help a small smile in return.

"I've brought you a visitor." She pushed the door wide and stepped inside, placing her bundle and rifle in the corner.

Elena scurried in behind her. After handing off the second bundle to Alejandra, Elena hastened to the bed and perched next to Mama Sarita, resting a hand on her shoulder. "I came to check on you, Señora. Is there anything I can do to help?"

The image pressed firmly on Alejandra's conscience. She should have been kinder to Elena. The woman had come to help. And it wasn't Elena's fault that her husband was still alive and well, despite all the other men dead.

No, Alejandra should rejoice with her friend that the babe's father lived, and they wouldn't be cast into the streets. The way Alejandra and Mama Sarita were about to be.

As soon as the mother and child left, Alejandra moved toward the stove. "What would you like for *la comida*?"

"No, mija. Come sit at the table with me. We must talk."

Alejandra spun to face Mama Sarita. Her voice held such a weight. Such dread, laced with determination. She didn't meet Alejandra's gaze, but motioned toward a chair at the table, as she settled into the one next to it.

Alejandra sank into the chair beside Mama Sarita. What now? Had something else happened?

"Mija. I have sought the Lord's guidance for our next direction."

Alejandra nodded, her mind churning with the information Elena had shared on the walk over. "Sí, Mama. Elena said there are jobs for women in Nuevo Laredo. We could work together as cooks maybe. I'll see if I can find a ride for us on a wagon."

Mama Sarita's hand settled on Alejandra's arm, stopping any further chatter. "That will be good for you, but do not seek a ride for me."

The words echoed in the quiet room, but couldn't penetrate the walls of Alejandra's understanding. "What?"

Paper shuffled as Mama Sarita raised a hand from her lap, displaying a stack of tattered letters. "I should go live with my sister."

Sister? Mama Sarita had never spoken of family before, save Papa Ricardo and Luis. If she had a sister, why didn't she speak of her? Why didn't the sister take part in all the holidays? *Familia* was so important to Mama Sarita.

And then a terrible thought struck her. Though she was Mexican in every way that mattered now, Mama Sarita had been raised in America. Is that where her sister still lived? It was too awful to even consider.

"Are...are you saying move to America?" Alejandra tightened her jaw, trying to still the quiver in her chin.

"Sí, mija. I must go home."

Home? The word struck Alejandra like a blow to her face. She grabbed Mama Sarita's hand and pulled it across the table to her own bosom. "But, Mama. This is your home. We must stay together. We have to." It didn't matter that her voice rose like a frightened horse in a barn fire.

Mama Sarita dropped the papers on the table, and brought her free hand up to cup Alejandra's cheek. "Alejandra. You are as dear to me as any daughter. Sí, my greatest wish was for you to marry my Luis and become my daughter truly. That cannot happen now, but you will always be in my heart.

"But a young woman like you has so many choices. I will help you find *el esposo*. A husband who will protect and cherish you as you deserve. As my own Luis would have done." The older woman's voice caught, and her rich brown eyes glistened.

16

"And when I am content your situation is good, I will go home to my sister. To Texas."

Alejandra clamped her teeth over her lower lip, holding in the sob that fought for release. No. None of it could be true. Everything about Mama Sarita's words was so wrong.

She couldn't marry yet. It was too soon after Luis's death. And Papa's. And she would not marry without love. She and Luis had been good companions. Her love for him was perhaps not as great as her love for his family. But she would not allow herself to be promised to another man for whom she had not even friendship.

And Texas? Mama Sarita couldn't leave. No. Not to another country. Even if it was the place she had grown up, how could Mama Sarita want to go back to the land of the soldiers who had killed her husband and son? The sob in Alejandra's chest broke free, loosening the tears she'd tried to hold back.

Mama Sarita pulled her into an embrace, clutching Alejandra's head to her shoulder and rocking. "Mija. My Alejandra." Over and over she murmured the endearments. Rocking. Holding. Letting Alejandra cry without shushing her.

At last the torrent of tears slowed enough for Alejandra to quench them. She sniffed and pulled back, wiping her eyes with the underside of her apron. "I'm sorry."

"Hush, mija. Don't apologize. Tears are healing and can bring clarity. I have cried many tears myself to reach this point."

Alejandra nodded. Her mind *was* clearer. There was no doubt now what she had to do. Inhaling a long breath, she met Mama Sarita's gaze. "You're sure you want to go to Texas?"

17

Nothing but love shone in the older woman's eyes, bolstering Alejandra even more. Her decision was right.

"Sí, mija. It's a little town there called Seguin. The people are good. I have prayed much and feel it's the Lord's will." Her hand closed in a fist over her heart.

"Okay, then. We will go."

Mama Sarita's forehead wrinkled, confusion turning the deep brown in her eyes murky. "You don't have to go with me. I understand your home is Mexico."

Alejandra forced resolve into her spine. She couldn't back down now. Placing her hand in the woman's dear, callused one, she kept her voice gentle but firm. "Mama Sarita, where you go, I will go. You're my only family left. I won't let you leave alone. I can't. Where you live will be my home also."

Mama Sarita's mouth pinched for a long moment, and the expression in her eyes bespoke a battle among her emotions. Finally, a corner of her lips quirked. Then the other side. Her eyes softened into the most radiant smile Alejandra had seen in days.

"My Alejandra." With those words, Mama pulled her into another embrace, squeezing with such fierce love, there could be no doubt of the emotion. Alejandra clung to her in return. Surely anything they would have to endure in America would be worth it, as long as they were together.

Right?

Chapter Three

ALEJANDRA wrapped the red shawl tighter around her shoulders and hunched underneath the pack on her back. They'd been walking for days now. She'd lost track of how many sunrises they'd seen on the trail, but it'd been more than a week since they rode the raft across the Rio Bravo and landed on Texas soil. With every day they traveled, the landscape became a little more lush, even though the grass had turned an early-December brown, and the trees were mostly skeletons. The air held a little more chill now, too.

A soft mew from behind brought Alejandra's head around. The cat sat on the road staring at her, as if it refused to take another step. Even though she carried him half the time, this trip had been hard on the little furball. "Come on, Rudy. Catch up." He released one more sad mew, as if making sure his complaint was documented, then scampered to catch up.

A movement at her side caught Alejandra's attention. Mama Sarita stumbled and gasped as she went down on one knee. Alejandra reached frantically, and snagged a handful of the woman's sleeve. She held on tight until Mama Sarita regained her balance, then rose to both feet.

"Are you hurt?" Alejandra bracketed her with a hand on each shoulder and peered into tired eyes.

"No. I stumbled on a rock. I'm all right."

She allowed a long breath to slow the wild beating in her chest. "I wish you would have let me buy a donkey for the trip. This is too far for you to walk, especially carrying a pack." Truth was, if she'd had enough money, she would have bought the donkey without Mama's consent. Even after all the things Mama Sarita had given away to neighbors, their belongings filled two large satchels. It was too much for the older woman to carry day after day.

"Mija, I'm old, but I'm not *decrépito*. The walking is good for me, and we'll save our money for our new life." She patted Alejandra's arm, then turned and strode off, her step a little jauntier than before. Was she trying to prove she was up to the challenge?

Alejandra sighed and forced her own heavy feet to move, lengthening her stride to catch up with the other woman. It would help if her legs weren't so short, especially compared to Mama Sarita's tall, willowy figure.

Ahead of her, Mama Sarita's head bobbed, and she listed sideways. Before Alejandra could leap forward, Mama was down on one knee, then rolling onto her side. The whole scene happened as if in a dream. One of those terrible dreams where Papa was falling over the edge of a cliff, and no matter how hard Alejandra pushed, she couldn't make her body move faster than a slow crawl. In the dreams, she would finally reach Papa just as his grip on the ledge loosened, and she would watch him writhe as he dropped down, down, down...

She landed on her knees at Mama Sarita's side, forcing the remnants of the dream out of her mind. "Mama!"

"I'm all right, mija." But her breath came hard and her words wrapped around a groan. The older woman's hand drifted down to her right leg.

"Where are you hurt? Your knee?"

Mama shook her head once. "My...foot." Her face scrunched, then she struggled to sit up.

"Lie still, Mama. Let me look at it."

But Mama Sarita pushed aside her words with a wave of her hand. Against her better judgment, Alejandra helped her sit up, then knelt by her feet and loosened the laces on her shoe. It was a homemade boot, constructed of a soft leather upper and several layers of thick cowhide for the sole. Or perhaps the leather had been stiff in the beginning, but had softened after many years of wear.

As she slid the shoe off, a moan crept out of Mama Sarita. Alejandra swallowed back her own cry as she peeled down the stocking and the puffy red flesh of the ankle glared up at her. A pale green seeped just under the skin. She'd not seen such a bad sprain since Papa'd been thrown from one of the younger saddle horses when an angry bull charged.

Alejandra raised her head to examine their surroundings. No houses in sight, and she couldn't remember

21

seeing any for at least ten or fifteen minutes now. Should she walk on ahead and try to find someone to help? There was no way Mama Sarita could hobble very far. Trees bordered the road just ahead. Should she try to settle Mama Sarita inside the woods so she'd be protected? That looked like the best option for now.

Alejandra gazed into her friend's pain-streaked eyes. "Do you think we can get you over to those trees?" She nodded toward the woods. "Then I'll go for help."

Mama nodded. "Yes. I think we're not far from San Antonio, maybe another mile or two. Just get me off the road, and I'll be fine."

She tucked Mama Sarita's arm around her neck, and together they hobbled the twenty paces to the edge of the tree line. As she was about to lower the older woman to the ground, a rustling noise sounded within the timber.

"Wait, Mama. I hear something." Alejandra held her breath as she listened. Could it be? Had luck finally smiled on them? "I think I hear water running ahead. Can you rest against this tree while I go see?"

Mama nodded and released Alejandra for the smooth bark of the maple tree. Deep lines formed around her eyes, and her lids hung half closed. Alejandra's heart clenched at the sight. She had to get her settled soon, but a cool stream would be the very best thing for Mama Sarita's swollen foot.

She dashed through the trees, as Rudy scampered along underfoot. "Move, gato." She grunted, side-stepping so as not to crush the animal. When a small stream appeared through the woods, she could have cheered.

But moving Mama Sarita to the spot proved agonizing. Not because the sweet woman complained, but because it was clear from the shaking in her hands and her heavy breathing that every step was pure torture.

After settling her with the swollen ankle submerged in the creek, Alejandra loosened Papa's rifle from where she'd tied it to her satchel. "I'll only go as far as I need to, until I find *el cabello* for you to ride. And *la comida* to eat."

Mama Sarita gripped Alejandra's arm, her strength surprising after what she'd endured in the last hour. "Do you remember the English words?"

"Sí. Horse *y* food." Alejandra pronounced each word as clearly as she could, forcing her mouth around the strange sounds. They'd practiced American words every day on this journey, but it had taken a day or two before Alejandra summoned any desire to learn the language of these people. How she wished now she'd worked harder to memorize everything Mama Sarita tried to teach her.

"Bueno." Mama Sarita nodded. "I mean…good. I must begin to speak more English to you. Don't stop at the houses you come to, but go into San Antonio and find a mercantile. You never know what kind of people you'll meet on the road, but a storekeeper will help you."

"Sí, Mama. I'll leave the rifle with you." She reached down to give Rudy a final pat. "Stay here, boy, and help Mama

Sarita." The cat meowed, brushing against the gathered blue fabric at the base of her skirt.

Alejandra left the wooded area with the solid bounce of pesos bumping against her side in the pocket of her skirt. Urgency pushed her forward, and soon she began to pass houses. The homes grew closer and closer together until stores filled the roadside. Each building seemed to be taller and more ornate than the last. Curved scrollwork or solid pillars decorated many of them, along with bright paint colors and elaborate signs. How could these people afford such luxury on the outside of the buildings? What must the insides look like?

The writing on the signs made no sense, but some of them had pictures, too. One showed a boot and another a dress, so Alejandra watched for a signed that showed some kind of food. But it was her nose that alerted her first. Never had she smelled anything as tantalizing as the aroma that poured from the squatty building just in front of her. Of course, it may not have smelled half as wonderful if she'd had anything at all to eat that day.

Her stomach rumbled like a weaned calf. Alejandra rested one hand over her midsection to still the noise, and peered through a window in the front of the building. It was crowded, with some people milling about, and many more sitting in groups at tables around the room. Was this a mercantile? It wasn't like any *los mercados* back home.

Just then, three men exited the building, and stood on the wood sidewalk for a moment. One man spoke, and the other two laughed. The man's words had come so quickly, Alejandra had no idea what he said. Maybe these men could tell her if this was a mercantile.

She took a single step forward, and gathered a breath with her courage. "Señors?"

All three men turned to stare at her. The man closest pinched his mouth into a smile that made her hands clammy. Like Señor Rodriquez, who Papa had warned her to stay away from. Best to ask her question and get away from them.

She pointed toward the building they'd just exited. "Es mercantile? Sí?"

The first man's smile widened, raising bumps on Alejandra's arms. He took a step closer, and she shuffled back. Her short legs didn't take her very far though, and he grabbed her arm. His hand clamped around her wrist, and Alejandra squealed. How dare this man touch her? She jerked back, but his hold was like a vice.

The others were around her now. Touching her arms. Her back. Her face. Alejandra twisted and fought against their hold, but they pressed in. Smothering. She bit and kicked at them, her boot making contact with flesh once.

American words spewed from the mouth of the man in front of her, and he pressed his face just inches from hers. Hot breath laced with the stench of tequila, suffocated, bringing up bile into her throat. This vile Americano would pay for his actions.

Gathering as much moisture as she could summon, she spit hard into his face. The man blinked, then his features glowed an ugly shade of red. In the next second, the air filled with shouts, and a hard object slammed into her left cheek. Pain radiated through Alejandra's head, and lightning bolts flashed across her vision. Another fist crashed into her eye.

A mighty explosion split the air, and the noises stopped abruptly. The hands dropped away from her body, and relief washed through her. But without the support of them, Alejandra's legs lost their strength. Her vision went fuzzy, and her knees hit the ground as her skirts collapsed around her.

Alejandra fought hard to stay awake. To make the world stop spinning around her. She held very still for a moment, her gaze focused on the ground while she willed her head to settle. A man's voice pierced the air above her, but she couldn't see what was happening. It took every ounce of concentration to focus her vision. Finally, the ground stopped spinning. Her head still ached, and her cheek burned, but she slowly raised her gaze to where the men stood above her.

But no one was there. She eased her head in both directions. Even through fuzzy vision, it was plain she was alone. Those three awful men were gone. What stopped them?

And then she saw him. Her eyes focused on a single cowboy, standing several paces away. He stood tall, with brown hair cut short and a leather vest over a clean blue shirt. But it was the look in his eyes that stopped her short. They sparkled, reflecting a genuine emotion. It almost looked like...kindness?

But she gave herself a mental shake. She would be loco to trust him after what those other desperados did. Biting her lip against the spinning, she slowly rose to her feet and faced the man.

"Hello." His voice was rich and held a tone that seemed to match the compassion in his gaze.

What should she say? Should she turn and run? The throbbing and spinning in her head wouldn't let her move fast. No doubt he would catch her if he really wanted to. And what about food and a horse for Mama Sarita?

The man took a step forward and spoke a short sentence in American. Try as she might, none of the words were familiar. Should she ask him to speak slower? Or dare she ask where the mercantile was? That hadn't worked so well with those other men.

He let loose another string of words she couldn't decipher. Alejandra shook her head, frustration building in her chest. Something about this man made her feel safe, but that wouldn't help if she couldn't understand a thing he said.

She thought back to some of the words Mama Sarita had taught her. Aha. Carefully shaping her mouth, she said, "No speak…American."

A light came over his face. As if she'd just told him food was meant to be eaten. He thought for a moment, then said, "¿Te duelen?"

Chapter Four

IF he'd turned into a horse in front of her, Alejandra may not have been any more surprised. He spoke Spanish? His accent wasn't perfect, but it wasn't bad. He'd obviously heard the language spoken quite a bit.

"¿Sí?" He took another step forward, creases lining his forehead. The action jerked Alejandra from her shock. What had he asked? If she'd been hurt?

She took her own step...backward. "No. No estoy dolido." Even if she *were* hurt, she sure wouldn't tell this man. She raised her chin a notch, but the action pulled at the tender skin on her cheek where the renegades had struck her.

"Eso es bueno. ¿Puedo ayudar a que llegue a casa?" He wanted to help her get home? If only that were possible. Alejandra's heart squeezed at the thought.

But maybe he could help her get the things she needed. Dare she trust him? She would have to take a chance on someone. And there was something about this man that seemed safe. But she'd make sure to keep her distance.

She met his gaze and answered in her native Spanish. "I'm looking for the mercantile. Can you direct me?"

His mouth quirked into a light smile. Not the scary kind that sent chills down to her toes, but a happy smile. Like he was glad she'd given him a chance to help.

He touched the brim of his hat and spoke again in perfect Spanish. "Sí, Señorita. I'd be honored to take you there."

Turning, he extended a hand in the direction from which she'd come. Had she passed the mercantile on her way into town? If that was the case, she really did need help, at least finding the building. With a wary eye on the man, Alejandra stepped forward and walked beside him on the boardwalk.

He seemed even taller now that he walked close. But his size was more comforting than unnerving. What was it about him that spoke confidence?

"Are you new to this area?" His Spanish was slow but easy to understand.

Her gaze shot to his face, and found him watching her. She jerked her focus back to the street in front of them. He kept to a leisurely stroll, but she still had to take long steps to keep up.

"Sí." Should she say anything more? No. It couldn't be safe to give any more details than necessary.

He seemed to accept her silence without resentment, though, and they walked past a few more buildings. Stopping in front of a tall, two-story structure, he opened the door and motioned for her to walk in.

"What are you looking for?" he asked in a low voice.

"La comida," she whispered back. The place was filled with shelves and displays and tables covered with more than Alejandra could have imagined. Boxes and bags and barrels lined one empty wall. And a table in the far corner held stacked rows of fabrics—more colors and designs than she'd seen in years.

The man motioned toward the other side of the large room. Jars lined a bookcase, and more large sacks sat on the floor. A small table draped with a bright red table cloth held loaves of bread and round containers that looked like they held cornbread cakes.

Alejandra's stomach rumbled. Loud enough for the whole store to hear, especially the cowboy standing mere feet away. *Don't look at him. Pretend nothing happened.* But her wayward gaze found his face—and the hint of a smile there.

"Sounds like we should head to the café for lunch after we leave here." His eyes twinkled. Was he laughing at her?

Alejandra tore her gaze away and strode forward to examine the bread on the table. "No. I have to get back to Mama Sarita."

He stood patiently while she examined each of the foods. Everything looked so good and just made her hungrier. Finally, she selected a loaf of bread, some dried meat, and cans of corn and tomatoes. Hopefully she would still have enough money to rent a horse, but they had to have food until they reached the town of Seguin and found Mama Sarita's sister. Mama had said it was still two or three days walk from this city.

She carried her parcels to the counter where the cowboy waited. As she set everything out, a tall man stepped up behind the counter and began making marks on a sheet of paper. The bare top of his head glimmered in the light from the lantern beside him, while a crown of pale yellow hair hung limp like fringe over his ears. His bright red vest barely buttoned around his expansive middle.

The man looked up and spoke something to her in American. She caught the word "cents," but nothing more. Alejandra fought back a frustrated groan. These people spoke so much faster than Mama Sarita when she was teaching Alejandra new words. Why did nothing sound familiar?

"He said the total cost is sixty cents." The cowboy spoke softly, and his words released the tension coiled in Alejandra's shoulders.

She pulled three coins from her skirt pocket. How many pesos was sixty cents? She laid two on the counter, then looked at the storekeeper.

He examined the coins for a moment and his brows knit, then he looked up and spat a stream of words at her. She didn't have to understand them to see the anger flaring in his eyes. The cowboy spoke to the round man in a low, commanding voice. Stronger than any he'd used with Alejandra.

The storekeeper addressed the cowboy again, his words more reluctant than angry this time. Alejandra understood only the word "money." The cowboy spoke again, determined patience slowing his words so she picked out "pay" and "cents." Was he bartering a lower price for the food? Alejandra bit back a smile. Luck had smiled on her when she met this man.

Finally, the storekeeper picked up one of her pesos and pushed the other back in her direction. He lifted the items into a small wooden crate, shoved it toward her, then spun and walked away without a word.

The cowboy turned toward her, a dissatisfied pinch lining his mouth, and spoke in her language. "He is sorry for his words." He reached for the crate, but Alejandra grabbed it first. Even though this man had been kind so far, she would hold onto her own possessions.

When they stepped outside, the man turned left onto the boardwalk in the direction they had come. He walked as if he expected her to stay with him. Where was he taking her? She needed to ask for directions to the livery, then it would be best to send him on his way.

Alejandra stopped, and a stride later he turned to look at her, brows raised.

"What's wrong?"

She squared her shoulders. "Please tell me where to find the livery, then I won't be a bother to you anymore."

Twin lines formed on his forehead. "Can I buy you lunch at the café first?"

This man wanted to give her food? No. That would be trusting him too much. And Mama Sarita waited. No, she wouldn't fill her stomach knowing Mama had not eaten yet today.

Shaking her head, Alejandra said, "No, Mama Sarita waits for me. I need to rent a horse and go back to her."

The cowboy's mouth pinched again, and he seemed reluctant as he turned back the way he had been walking. "The livery is this way."

Alejandra scurried to catch up with him, then settled into his relaxed stride.

Several moments passed before he spoke again. "Can you ride a horse?"

Alejandra's gaze jerked to him. Couldn't everyone? "Sí, but the horse is for Mama Sarita to ride."

He glanced at her with one brow raised. "Can *she* ride a horse?"

"Sí."

The way his eyes danced when he smiled was captivating. "The livery owner will need to know how long you plan to keep the horse."

Oh. She hadn't thought about how to bring the horse back to this town. Maybe after Mama Sarita was settled with her sister, Alejandra could bring the horse back, then walk to Seguin again. She nibbled her lower lip. How long would that take? Maybe this cowboy would know of the town.

"Señor, do you know how far to Seguin?"

The man's eyes widened. "Seguin? Your madre is going to Seguin?"

No need to correct his misunderstanding of her relationship with Mama Sarita, but why did he seem surprised about the town? "Sí. We're both going. Do you know how far?"

He seemed to recover himself. "It's about thirty miles. A long day's ride." He paused for a moment. "So you need two horses?"

"No. Mama Sarita rides because her foot is injured. I will walk."

Those two lines formed on his forehead again, but the man didn't answer. In fact, he remained silent as they passed two more buildings, then stopped in front of an open barn door.

EDWARD straightened his spine as he stepped through the wide livery door, the woman by his side. Something about her drew him in a way no other woman had. She was beautiful, to be sure. Even with streaks of dirt gracing her cheeks and jaw, her tiny features and dark eyes took his breath every time he looked at her.

It's a good thing he found her when he did. Goose bumps covered his arms every time he thought about what those lowlifes would have done with her. No woman deserved that, especially not this delicate flower beside him.

Edward scanned the barn aisle. "Malcolm?"

A head of red curls poked from a stall like a gopher from a hole in the ground. "Yep?" Recognition dawned, and he stepped out of the stall and strode toward them with long, lanky steps. "Edward. Good to see you, chap." Turning to the woman, he placed a hand across his midsection and bent slightly in a half bow. "Hallo, miss." Malcolm's tone picked up a hint of his Scottish ancestry as he spoke the words.

"Malcom, this lady needs to rent a buggy or wagon for a week or two. What do you have for her?"

The man's thick red brows lowered until they covered half his eyes. "Afraid all my buggies are out right now, 'scept the Doc's, but I can't give you that." His brows rose again as he turned to Edward. "Will a wagon do?"

Edward gave a single nod. "Fine. I'll settle up with you once we get the lady on her way. Good?"

Malcolm spun and charged his lanky form back down the aisle. "I'll have 'em ready afore you can sneeze. Meet you around front."

Edward bit back a smile at his friend's enthusiasm. Turning to the woman at his side, something in his stomach tightened at the sight. She nibbled her lower lip again. It was the cutest habit, one she appeared to do any time she was thinking or worried. And this time it looked to be worry. A single line marred the beautiful skin of her forehead. Everything in him wanted to take away whatever it was that concerned her.

He lowered his voice to a gentle tone and switched to Spanish. "He's gone to hitch a team to the wagon."

Her dark eyes widened into horror. "No! No wagon. I can only afford a horse. Or a donkey. No wagon." Her words tumbled out so quickly he had to focus to interpret the steady barrage.

Out of instinct, he reached to settle a hand on her shoulder. Something to calm her down. But the anger that sparked in her eyes as she leaped backward made him jerk his hand away quicker than a snake could strike.

"Don't worry." He kept his voice calm, but his mind reeled faster than a thrown lariat. And then an explanation came to him.

"You don't have to pay. The owner needs the wagon delivered to the livery in Seguin, so he would consider it a favor if you drove it there. No charge." His conscience revolted at the lie, but what else could he say? He had to get her to take the wagon. Seguin was way too far to walk, and it didn't seem like she would accept a gift. An innocent lie couldn't hurt if it was spoken to help someone, right? The same way he'd added her food to his tab at the mercantile when ol' Harry refused to accept her Mexican coin. But still, an uneasy weight settled over him.

The expression on her face changed to wary scrutiny. Would she accept the gift? His chest tightened as he waited.

A slight nod of her cute pointed chin gave her decision. Tension slid from Edward's body as he watched the movement. The relief that flowed through him was a little unnerving. Why did it matter so much to him what happened to this woman? Sure, she was beautiful, and vulnerable, and obviously in need of help. Maybe he was so protective because he came upon her when those thugs attacked. If he could be assured she and her mother had a safe ride to Seguin, with food to eat until they

36

arrived, that would be enough. But what would they do when they got there?

He chose his words carefully. "Are you going to visit family in Seguin?"

She nodded. "Mama Sarita's sister lives there with her husband."

Another wave of relief. "My sister and her husband own a ranch outside of town. Perhaps I'll see you there sometime."

The sound of a wagon outside the open doorway grabbed Edward's attention, and he led the woman toward the team as Malcom stepped down from the seat. She scrambled up before he could do more than touch her elbow.

"You know how to drive a rig, ma'am?" Malcolm eyed her.

She didn't answer, but looked at him with that line creasing her forehead again.

With a jolt, Edward realized she didn't understand. He quickly translated. Never before had he been so thankful for all the Spanish he'd learned from the cowboys on his brother-in-law's ranch. He'd be hard-pressed to find a better group of vaqueros.

Upon hearing the question, the woman turned a radiant smile on Malcolm and took up the reins. She responded in Spanish. "Sí. Papa taught me many skills with horses. I'll deliver the wagon to Seguin as you ask."

A pinch of jealousy snagged Edward at the smile she aimed toward the liveryman. But the effect it had on the fellow was a bit funny. Red crept up his neck and into his cheeks, almost matching the orangeish red of his beard and hair.

"What'd she say, chap?" He spoke out of the side of his mouth in a low tone, as his gaze dropped to where his boot toed the ground

Edward couldn't help himself. "She said her pa taught her all about horses. And she said she wouldn't let an old Scott like you show her anyway."

The man's head shot up. For a second, he stared at Edward. Then a slow smile spread across his face. "You're a hoot, Stewart. She didn't say that any more'n you spoke German."

He allowed his own grin to break free as he clapped Malcom on the shoulder. "You're right. But she did say her Pa taught her to drive a team. I think she'll be fine."

Malcolm looked up at the woman again, then back at Edward. "All right, then. Reckon I'll be inside if you need anything." He gave the lady another half bow. "Good day, ma'am."

When he was gone Edward stepped closer to the wagon and rested his hand on the corner. He spoke in Spanish. "Is there anything else I can help you with in town? I'd take you to Seguin myself, but I'm supposed to report for work this afternoon here in San Antonio."

Her chin dipped as her mouth spread into a shy smile. "You've done too much already. I thank you for your kindness."

He had to fight his reflexes so he didn't reach up and stroke the delicate skin of her cheek. He had to get control of himself. What if he never saw this woman again? He had to report for another assignment today, so it would be days or even a week before he got back to Seguin. But he'd look her up for sure.

And then a thought struck him. He gazed into those beautiful dark eyes. "I don't know your name."

Her lips pulled into a teasing smile and her eyes danced. "Alejandra Diaz."

Alejandra. It rolled off her lips like an exotic song. Everything about this woman was intoxicating.

"And you are?"

Like a simple-minded dog he stood there looking at her. He reached up to tip his hat, then realized it wasn't there. Instead he offered a lazy salute. "Edward Stewart, Miss Diaz. It's been a pleasure to meet you."

She rewarded him with that same radiant smile she'd given Malcolm. His heartbeat sped up and his stomach did an extra flip.

"I thank you, Señor Stewart. You've been most kind. I'll bid you adios now."

With that, she gave the reins a strong shake. The horses stepped into the harness, pulling the wagon forward.

"Adios," Edward called. Something in his chest constricted, as he watched her drive down the road and out of sight.

Chapter Five

REINING the horses to a stop beside the trees that sheltered Mama Sarita, Alejandra set the wagon brake and jumped to the ground. This blue skirt didn't billow like her brown one did, letting her move more freely.

Carrying the bread and meat, she wove through the trees until she reached the river. Mama Sarita sat with her eyes closed and foot extended into the water. Her lids flickered open when Alejandra dropped to her knees beside the older woman.

"I brought food and a wagon. Eat some now, then more while we travel."

"Gracias, Dio," Mama Sarita whispered the prayer, as she took the bread Alejandra offered. The woman's eyes studied Alejandra's face while she ate, halting at her left eye. "Mija," she breathed, reaching to almost touch the aching skin. "What happened?"

Alejandra gulped. "It's nothing. Some people weren't friendly, but a kind man helped, and I have what we need now."

"Mija." The word repeated, sounded almost like a groan this time.

Alejandra looked around for a distraction. Mama Sarita had enough heartache without worrying about that. "Tell me when you're ready to go."

"I am ready."

Strapping the rifle over her shoulder, Alejandra rewrapped the leftover food, then helped Mama Sarita stand and hobble through the trees. As they walked, she scanned the area for the cat. No gray ball of fur scampered beside them, so she raised her voice to call. "Ru-dy!" Nothing.

Mama Sarita hobbled slower now, her face contorted into a grimace. But they were almost to the road.

Once they reached the wagon, Mama Sarita held onto the side while Alejandra laid blankets in the bed. They worked together to lift Mama Sarita and her very swollen ankle up into the conveyance. By the time she lay back against the blankets, much of the color had drained from her tanned face.

Alejandra stroked hair from the older woman's face. "I'll get Rudy, then we'll move on. Hopefully you can sleep while I drive."

"Gracias." The word was faint, and Mama Sarita's eyelids had already drifted shut.

Alejandra retraced their steps to the stream, calling her wayward cat every few seconds. Where could he be? He was normally underfoot, always wanting to be close to her. She'd never been concerned he'd run away.

At the water, she paused to scan the bank in each direction. "Ru-dy!" Something moved upriver, rustling the leaves as it scampered near a tree. Her heart picked up speed, but then the animal stepped away from the tree. Only a squirrel.

She walked that direction anyway, calling Rudy's name as she went. What should she do if she didn't find the cat soon? Leave him? That would mean one more loved one lost. Moisture stung her eyes. Why was life so hard?

Maybe they could spend the night here, and give Rudy time to come back? But Mama Sarita needed a doctor. She surely didn't need to sleep out in the woods with her foot swollen. And they wouldn't have enough food if they didn't leave for Seguin today.

After walking for several minutes, she came to a break in the trees. In the clearing sat a tall farmhouse, at least two levels high and painted white. Could Rudy be there? Dare she go ask if they'd seen him?

But what had Mama Sarita said? *Don't stop at the houses you come to, but go into San Antonio and find a mercantile. You never know what kind of people you'll meet on the road, but a storekeeper will help you.*

Considering the kind of men she'd met in town, how much worse would people living out here be? She couldn't chance it. Retreating back into the woods, Alejandra followed the stream back to where she'd started, still calling the cat every few moments. As she trudged through the woods back to the wagon, the tears finally broke through her lashes. Her precious cat, and one of her last two friends. Gone...

THE next morning, Alejandra drove the wagon through the gateway of the solid wall around the little town of Seguin.

Mama Sarita released a contented sigh beside her. "We're here, mija. We've finally made it."

It'd been a long night getting here, but to have Mama Sarita in a safe place where she could recover from her injury would be worth it. This town was smaller than San Antonio, but the one- and two-story buildings were still nicer than most she'd seen in Mexico. Except maybe the casa grande where the Don and Doña lived at Rancho Las Cuevas. That had been a huge, two-story structure that sprawled over an enormous plot of ground. With courtyards and gardens, and everything extravagant.

The homes that lined the street were attractive, but not too showy or vulgar. As they drove farther, signs hung from the fronts of some of the buildings, and a few people strolled along the wooden walkway that lined the street.

"Mama Sarita, do you know which is your sister's home?"

Mama's lips pinched as she examined first one side of the street, then the other. "No. I've not seen their new home. In her letters, she said they live above their store." She pressed a hand on Alejandra's arm. "Here, stop the wagon and let me ask these women."

Alejandra obeyed as Mama Sarita spoke to the ladies in American. One was an older woman, her hair white-gray with a few dark streaks. The other was a little younger, maybe a few years older than Mama Sarita.

Both women's faces lit up when they heard Mama Sarita's question. The younger smiled and pointed down the road as she jabbered something Alejandra couldn't understand. She was really going to have to work on her American. Even if she couldn't speak much, she needed to be able to understand what was being said around her.

Mama Sarita spoke to the ladies again and waved. Alejandra picked out the words "Thank you," before Mama Sarita turned to her.

"They said it's the second to last building on the left side of the street. The name 'Stewart Mercantile' is over the door."

Alejandra nodded as she slapped the reins on the horses' backs, and they started off.

The building was just where the women had said, a two-story structure built of the same white adobe-like material as many of the other structures. Alejandra reined in the team beside the mercantile, then jumped down and turned to help Mama Sarita. Instead, the woman held out a letter.

"Here. Take this inside and show it to whoever is behind the counter. Tell them to *come outside*." Mama Sarita used the American words "come outside," sounding them slowly.

Alejandra took the paper and strode toward the door, repeating the two words over and over in her mind. She would learn the American language if it killed her.

A bell on the door tinkled as Alejandra opened it, and her eyes immediately found a tall, broad man behind the counter on the left side of the room. The rest of the open room was similar to the mercantile in San Antonio, but not as large. It was early in the day still, and no other customers were there.

"Howdy, Miss." The man had a booming voice, but at least she was able to understand those two words.

She stepped toward the counter, picking her way around a table stacked with cans. "Señor." Holding the letter out like a sign, her mouth formed the American words. "Come outside, por favor."

The lines on his forehead deepened as he took the letter and examined the writing on the front.

"Come outside," she said again, this time pointing in the direction she'd come.

A light dawned in his eyes. He seemed to understand what she wanted him to do, and his face held a curious half-smile. He said something Alejandra couldn't understand as he strode around the edge of the counter and motioned for her to precede him.

Alejandra released her breath as she scurried toward the door, where Mama Sarita waited. Alejandra went to stand next to Mama Sarita's side of the wagon and watched the man.

He stopped on the boardwalk, and raised a hand to shade his eyes as he took in the two of them and the wagon. It was clear the instant he recognized Mama Sarita. His eyes grew into round circles, even under the shadow of his palm. He took a tentative step forward. "Sara?" His voice held wonder, as if he might be seeing a vision.

"Hello, Walter." Emotion spilled out of Mama Sarita's tone.

"Sara," he breathed again. He stepped back and it looked like he would turn and hurry inside, but then he changed direction and strode toward the wagon. "Let me help you down. Your sister will have my head if I wait one more second before I bring you in."

"Wait." The single word from Mama Sarita stopped him in his tracks at the base of the wagon, and he raised the hand to his eyes again to shield them from the Eastern sun.

"What's wrong?" Walter's booming voice was laced with concern.

Mama Sarita answered him, but the only words Alejandra could pick out were "hurt," "Laura," and "here." The man spun on his heel and disappeared back in the shop.

Mama's eyes sparkled when she turned to smile at Alejandra. "He's gone to bring Laura. You'll like her, mija. She's one of the sweetest creatures God put on this earth."

The joy that lit Mama Sarita's face as she described her sister made Alejandra's heart constrict. One wicked part of her regretted having to share Mama's love, even with her own sister. But her nobler side couldn't wait to meet the woman of whom such good things could be spoken.

46

They didn't have to wait long. Footsteps inside gave warning just before the front door burst open and a tall, willowy woman bounded out.

"Sara!" The woman—who could only be Laura Stewart—had Mama Sarita in an embrace almost before Alejandra could step out of the way. The sisters laughed and cried and hugged for almost a full minute as Alejandra and Laura's husband looked on. Then Mama Sarita leaned back from her sister's embrace and wiped her eyes. She gathered Laura's hand in her left, and reached for Alejandra with her right hand.

She said something to her sister in English, with the words "daughter" and "Alejandra." Then she turned to Alejandra and bestowed a smile filled with such love, Alejandra wanted to spring into her arms. But instead she listened as Mama Sarita said in Spanish, "Mija, I'd like you to meet my sister Laura and her husband Walter."

Laura stepped forward then, and wrapped Alejandra in her arms. Her words weren't distinguishable, but the warmth in her hug was clear.

THE next morning, Alejandra was elbow-deep in wash water as she scrubbed a frying pan and listened to strings of American words fly back and forth between the sisters. Tía Laura—as she insisted Alejandra call her—stood beside her with a clean cloth, drying and putting the dishes away after Alejandra cleaned them. Mama Sarita sat in a chair by the table with her swollen foot propped in a second chair.

As they worked, Tía Laura rattled on about something to do with a "store" and a "baby." Alejandra allowed her gaze to travel around the small room as it had done more than once since they'd arrived yesterday. This was so much nicer than the adobe huts with dirt floors they'd lived in at Rancho Las Cuevas. And in the bedroom where she and Mama Sarita had slept, there was a real mirror, the mattress sat on some kind of wood contraption that kept it off the floor, and there had been soft cotton squares filled with goose down for them to lay their heads on. She'd not slept so well in years.

A laugh from Mama Sarita broke through Alejandra's thoughts. As the laughter faded, Mama Sarita spoke in Spanish. "Mija, my sister asks if you'd like to go with her on her errands this morning. She's going to the meat market, so maybe you can choose a pork haunch to make tamal de cerdo for the meal tonight. We need to teach Laura and Walter an appreciation for our Mexican food." Pleasure emanated from her tone, and Alejandra couldn't bring herself to say no.

"Sí. I'll go." But that didn't mean she was looking forward to going out into this strange town with a woman who didn't speak her language. At least together they should be safer than Alejandra had been alone in San Antonio.

An hour later, Alejandra found herself taking quick steps beside Tía Laura's long strides. It was warm for a December day, but Alejandra still pulled her red shawl tight around her shoulders. Many more people traversed the streets today than she'd seen from the wagon yesterday. A strange mixture of people, young and old, some with light skin like Tía Laura, and others with dark skin the color of a sorrel horse. Alejandra tried not to stare, but she'd never seen people quite like them.

At the next shop, Tía Laura motioned for Alejandra to follow her inside. The inside was dark and stank of raw meat, but Tía Laura didn't seem to notice as she strolled along the glass counter. She greeted the man behind the counter, and only then did Alejandra notice he, too, had dark ebony skin like some of the people she'd seen on the street.

He returned the greeting with a smile, and his bright white teeth shown in the dim light of the room. Alejandra couldn't quite pull her eyes away from him. As he and Tía Laura completed their business, his voice rolled in a lilting accent. It was pleasant to hear, but she couldn't understand anything he said. Not a word.

Outside again, Tía Laura named several buildings as they passed, offering a word or two of explanation if the occupation wasn't clear by the name. The International Hotel pricked Alejandra's interest right away. Might they have any work for her? What was the American word for someone who cleaned a house or hotel? She'd have to wait until she learned how to say them from Mama Sarita before she inquired at the hotel.

A middle-aged woman holding a child's hand passed them on the sidewalk and flashed them both a wide smile. The people here were so kind, even if some of them did look a little strange. Maybe they'd come to a good place after all. A place where she and Mama Sarita could start a new life.

Something flashed across the street. Just the glimmer of sunshine on metal, but it grabbed Alejandra's attention. A wagon passed, obstructing her vision for a few seconds. When it moved on, her heart froze. The sun had glinted on metal pinned to the shirt of a man. Tall and burly, with dark hair covering his face. And a gun hanging from his side. *El Soldado*.

Even in this town that seemed so friendly, they hadn't escaped the presence of soldiers. Alejandra gripped the package in her hands tighter and lengthened her stride. Soldiers had killed Mama, Papa, Luis, and Papa Ricardo. There was no way she'd let them separate her from Mama Sarita.

No way.

ALEJANDRA slid the brush through the long coffee-colored strands of Mama Sarita's coarse hair, as they prepared to start the day. With all the tangles gone, she wove her fingers through, melding the hairs into a secure plat at the nape of her neck.

How should she make her request this morning? *Mama Sarita, I feel I'm a burden to your sister and her husband. Won't you please let me inquire about a job at the hotel?* That hadn't worked the first time, nor any of the other days this past week since she'd first seen the sign at The International Hotel. But maybe today Mama Sarita would consent.

She gathered her nerve and tried to keep her voice casual as she asked, "Mama Sarita, do you mind if I leave you for a short time this morning to inquire about work at the hotel?"

Mama flicked her hand in a careless wave. "There will be time for that later. Today we go to see my sister's niece. Anna lives on a ranch outside of town and is great with child. She's about your age, I think. Or maybe a little older." Mama Sarita turned to pat Alejandra's cheek. "You will like her, mija. It's good for you to meet new friends."

Alejandra inhaled a breath to calm her clenched muscles. Friends she could do without. Work she needed. "How long will we be gone? Perhaps I can go to The International when we return?"

Mama Sarita's shoulders raised in a slight shrug. "I can't say. My sister said it's two hours to the ranch. Let's just go and enjoy the day with our new friends. Sí? We'll worry about the other when the Lord directs." And with that, Mama rose and tied an apron around her slender waist, signaling an end to the discussion.

Alejandra turned to the window as she fought back tears. Why was Mama Sarita being so difficult about this? Didn't she understand they needed to build their own life in this new land? Did she really want to rely on the hospitality of others for the rest of her life? Alejandra couldn't live that way.

The door clicked closed behind her, and Alejandra released a shaky sigh, then stood to don her own apron. She'd already started coffee on the stove before coming back to help Mama Sarita dress. She usually loved the special time each morning with Mama Sarita, but not today. Somehow she had to find a way to convince the older woman....

Chapter Six

WOULD she ever understand enough of the American language to follow a conversation? Words flowed around the breakfast table that morning, and from what Alejandra was able to pick up, it seemed the topic focused on their upcoming visit to the ranch. Mama Sarita would sometimes turn to Alejandra to interpret an important comment, so she could keep up. But for the most part, she found herself studying the faces of each person when they spoke. Each time Tía Laura mentioned Anna's name, a warmth settled over her face and voice, and her smile shown in her eyes.

When the meal ended, Alejandra began scrubbing dishes. Around her, clean-up and preparations for the outing took place in a whirl of bustling skirts and rapid-fire strings of American words.

Not thirty minutes after she stood from the breakfast table, Alejandra found herself seated on the outside edge of a wagon bench, with Mama Sarita in the middle, and Tía Laura

53

perched on the other end, holding the heavy leather reins. She drove the team like a woman on a mission, clicking her tongue and snapping the reins if the horses slowed.

The sun had just risen high enough to break through the winter gray, when they turned off the road at a lone fencepost onto a smaller dirt track. A house nestled in the distance, with a barn and a few other buildings nearby. Lines of wood fence spread out from the structures like ant trails in the sand. They crisscrossed each other in funny shapes, with some sort of animals inside—probably horses.

A man met them when they pulled into the ranch yard. Underneath a wide-brimmed sombrero, his black hair was tied with a strap, revealing deep lines in his leathery face. Such a face could only have come from a lifetime of hard work in the Southern sun. The lines creased deeper when he smiled in greeting. "Laura. Is good to have you visit."

His accent made the American words easier to understand, and the familiar angle of his features started a bubble of excitement in Alejandra. This man hailed from Mexico. The first countryman she'd met since arriving in Seguin.

He bowed slightly to Mama Sarita and Alejandra, a twinkle lighting his dark eyes. "Señora. Señorita. Señora O'Brien será tan feliz de tener que visite."

Alejandra could have jumped down and hugged the man. Finally, someone besides Mama Sarita who could speak words she understood. She'd never take such a blessing lightly again.

54

She responded in Spanish, with a pleasant nod. "Thank you, Señor. We are looking forward to our visit with Señora O'Brien."

As soon as he helped them down from the wagon, the man led the horses away, and Tía Laura herded them all toward the front door. The home was larger than it looked from the road, with two levels and a wide porch spanning the front.

Tía Laura pushed the door open without knocking. "Anna? Emmaline?" She stepped inside a long hall, untying her cloak as she gazed around.

A clatter of footsteps echoed from one of the rooms, and a tiny whirlwind of brown hair and blue fabric burst from a side doorway, flying into Tía Laura's arms.

"My Emmy-girl!" Tía Laura squeezed the child tight, then held her at arm's length. "Emmaline, I'd like you to meet my sister, Mrs. Sara, and Miss Alejandra."

The child turned to them, her chin dipping toward her chest, creating the cutest folds in her neck. Alejandra had to pinch her skirt so she didn't reach forward and tweak the adorable little button nose. The child couldn't be more than four or five. As cute as she was, though, it was the girl's eyes that were truly spectacular. A clear crystal blue, the color of the sky on a spring day. "Hello." Her voice dropped to a mouse-like level.

Alejandra squatted to meet the girl's gaze. "Hello, Emmaline." If only she knew more American words to speak to the child.

But she was saved the effort by a female voice calling from one of the side rooms. "Emmaline?"

The child came alive, babbling non-stop as she took Tía Laura's hand and led her in the direction of the voice. Alejandra glanced at Mama Sarita, who shrugged and followed her sister.

They entered a large room with several comfortable chairs positioned in a half-circle around a massive stone fireplace. A woman struggled to rise from a double-wide chair, her round belly protruding so she could only stand by pushing herself away from the chair seat.

Tía Laura scurried to the woman, who must certainly be Anna, and enveloped her in a hug. When she pulled back, Tía Laura bent down to Anna's swollen abdomen, speaking softly. It was such a tender moment, Alejandra had to swallow a lump in her throat.

Anna looked past her aunt and smiled at Mama Sarita and Alejandra, then said something. Tía Laura jumped in, and rattled off a string of American words. Alejandra smiled politely anytime someone spoke her name or pointed to her. The dialogue moved too fast, though, for her to keep up with the conversation. Would she ever be more than an outsider?

Mama Sarita, in her everlasting kindness, must have sensed Alejandra's frustration. She turned to speak in Spanish. "Anna says the child inside her has moved a lot lately. She is sure it must be a boy."

"Sí," said Anna, her eyes brightening as Spanish rolled off her tongue. "Él es grande y activa, al igual que su papá."

Alejandra stared at the woman, then closed her open jaw. Anna spoke almost perfect Spanish. But how? She looked so…American.

"How is it you speak Spanish?" Alejandra finally asked in her native tongue.

Anna smiled, laughter lighting her brown eyes. "Most of our ranch hands are from Mexico. Juan and the others have taught me much over the last ten years."

A smile parted Alejandra's lips, too, and she didn't try to hold it back. Two people now who could speak her own language. It was a good thing she came to visit this ranch after all.

Anna reached for Alejandra's hand and led her to the couch. She had to let go so she could use both hands to lower herself. But when Anna was settled, she patted the seat next to her. "Come and tell me about yourself, Alejandra Diaz. In which part of Mexico did you live?"

Time moved without notice, as Anna peppered Alejandra and Mama Sarita with questions. None of it seemed like prying, though. How could it when such innocent interest widened her eyes?

It wasn't long before Emmaline started to squirm in the chair beside her mother. Tía Laura rose and spoke something to Anna in American, then extended a hand to the little girl, and they left the room.

Anna turned back to Alejandra with an apologetic tilt to her mouth. "My aunt says she's going to have to learn Spanish to join our conversations."

Oh my. The last thing Alejandra wanted to do was displease Tía Laura. She started to ask Anna to call her back, but the woman placed a hand on Alejandra's arm. "She was teasing. Emmaline misses her aunt, so they've gone to prepare lunch together."

Mama Sarita scooted to the edge of her seat. "I should go try to help, too. Or is there something else I can do, Anna? Housework or laundry?"

Anna shook her head, but a double line pinched her brow. "Our neighbors' daughter has been coming to help after school. We get enough done to keep things around here working. My husband, Jacob, keeps telling me I need to hire a full-time helper to handle either the house or cooking for the vaqueros. I just can't bring myself to do it, though." A soft smile touched her lips. "Cooking for the men is why I came to the ranch all those years ago. It's special to me."

Mama Sarita rose, releasing a tiny groan as her limbs unfolded. "I'll go see what I can do to help my sister then."

Alejandra started to join her, but Anna pressed a hand to her arm. "Stay and visit with me. Please? I haven't had company in so long, and I can't get out like I used to."

Anna's face looked so hopeful, it forced down the guilt of sitting while the older women worked.

Alejandra nodded. "Sí. I am happy to talk to you."

They chatted for a while longer until a tantalizing aroma captured Alejandra's senses. She stopped in the middle of her question to Anna about how much land the ranch covered. "Do you smell that? I think Mama Sarita's made her famous chicken tortilla soup."

Before Anna could respond, the front door opened and boot thumps echoed in the hallway.

"Who is it?" Anna called in American, as she watched the open doorway.

A man strode through it, tall and lean and dressed like a vaquero, with a leather vest over his long work shirt. He said something in American as he strode toward Anna. A smile lit his crystal blue eyes as he gazed at her. No doubt about it, this had to be Emmaline's father. Anna's husband. Her suspicion was confirmed when he leaned over Anna and lowered his mouth to hers.

Alejandra turned away to give the couple privacy. And to fight the moisture building in her eyes. Would she and Luis have been like this, if he'd lived longer? He'd never looked at her the way Señor O'Brien looked at Anna. But Luis *had* seemed to enjoy being with her. Now she would never know.

Anna's voice broke through Alejandra's thoughts. In Spanish, the other woman said, "Jacob, I'd like you to meet Alejandra Diaz. She just moved here from Mexico with Aunt Laura's sister, Mama Sarita."

Señor O'Brien smiled from his place beside Anna's seat, as he answered in Spanish. "It's a pleasure to meet you, Señorita Diaz. Any friend or family of Walter and Laura is always welcome here."

Alejandra allowed a smile to bloom over her face. So many people that spoke her language here. "Thank you, Señor."

SEÑOR O'Brien joined them for the midday meal. But he left again soon after, and Mama Sarita urged her sister to leave the kitchen and spend time with Anna and little Emmaline. While they cleaned the dishes in the kitchen, Alejandra eyed the room. Dust and leaves had gathered on the floor in the corners, and rings of dried liquid marred the smooth surface of the table against the wall.

"Mama Sarita, do you think Anna would mind if I swept and wiped the tables? Should I ask her?"

A smile lit Mama's face. "I was just thinking the same. Poor girl is so big with child, the cleaning is hard. We'll do all we can, and let it be a surprise."

They set to the tasks, but it was amazing how cleaning such a grand house didn't feel like work. Alejandra had swept all the downstairs rooms, dusted the furniture and drapes, and emptied ashes from the stoves, by the time Mama Sarita began preparations for the evening meal.

"Can I help you, Mama?" Alejandra asked as she tucked the whisk broom into a corner of the storage room off the kitchen.

"Sí, mija. We'll have beef tamales tonight, with *frijoles refritos*. And maybe we can find some dried pears or apples for sweet tamales after the meal. Will you shred the meat while I cook the peppers?"

They worked for over an hour, preparing the food in tandem. They made such a great team, she and Mama Sarita. Warm, spicy aromas filled the house, bringing Tía Laura, Anna, and Emmaline in to peek at the food.

"Those tamales look amazing," Anna said in Spanish. "I've never been able to make mine stay wrapped in such neat bundles. The men are going to beg you to come cook for them every day."

Mama Sarita dismissed her comment with a wave. "Not at all. But we've made plenty so they can take some for the noon meal tomorrow." She stepped back from the work counter to examine the food laid out there. "I think we are almost ready. Just the table to prepare. How many places should we set?"

Anna's brows scrunched. "Let's see, there are sixteen men including Jacob and my brother. Plus the five of us ladies." A merry grin spread over her face. "It's a good thing our table is so large."

The lines deepened on Mama Sarita's forehead. "Alejandra and I can eat here in the kitchen." She motioned to the round table by the wall. "We don't want to crowd your family."

"Absolutely not. You're honored guests in our home. If I thought there wasn't room I would let Emmaline eat early. But that's not the case."

"What's not the case?" A deep voice resonated from the dining room, and moments later Señor O'Brien appeared in the kitchen doorway.

"I was telling Mama Sarita and Alejandra we wouldn't dream of letting them eat alone in the kitchen. There's plenty of room at the big table for us all."

Señor O'Brien's brows lowered and his blue eyes darkened. "Of course there's room. You'll eat in the dining room with all of us." Then his face softened. "You're family, after all."

As he left the room, Alejandra set back to work organizing the apple tamales on a clean tray, so they would be ready after the meal. Without warning, a rumbling sounded, along with the bang of wood on wood from the front of the house. The floor beneath her vibrated, and it took her a few moments to realize the rumble was the thud of many boots in the hallway. Tiny clinking noises sounded from the shelf where the serving dishes were stacked, as they, too, started to vibrate. Was this the vaqueros coming in for the evening meal? How did the house stand up to so many men filing through every day?

Anna stuck her head in the door. "Alejandra, we're ready to sit down for the blessing."

"Sí. Coming now." She settled the last two tamales on the tray, wiped her hands on her apron, and scurried toward the door.

The dining room hummed with conversation as some of the men stood and others settled into chairs. After a quick glance around to find Mama Sarita, Alejandra dipped her gaze and tried to be as invisible as possible while she slipped toward the seat where the woman motioned. What a relief to be seated between Mama Sarita and Tía Laura.

Señor O'Brien cleared his throat, and conversation quieted, replaced by the scraping of chairs as all the men settled in. They bowed their heads almost in unison, and Señor O'Brien offered a prayer in American.

Alejandra pressed her eyes closed, trying to understand some of the words. She was getting used to a prayer being spoken before each meal, since Tía Laura and Tío Walter followed the same tradition every time they sat down to eat. Señor O'Brien spoke some of the same things Tío Walter did, but the earnestness with which he said "Thank you" and "Father" made each word seem so heartfelt.

He ended with "Amen," and after she made the sign of the cross on her chest, Alejandra peeked around her lashes to make sure everyone else had opened their eyes. The last thing she wanted to do was offend these people by appearing irreverent if they had any strange customs after prayers.

When she did raise her head, she scanned the faces around the room. Anna was right, most of the vaqueros were Mexican.

And then her gaze skidded to a stop.

That face. *That man.* She blinked to clear her vision. Could it be him? It had to be. As if he could feel her gaze on him, he glanced up from the tamale on his plate, and a slow grin spread over his handsome face.

The cowboy from San Antonio. Edward Stewart.

Chapter Seven

FOR a long moment, they stared at each other. What was he doing here? Had he said something about working at a ranch outside of Seguin? Maybe—now that she thought about it. His deep brown eyes held hers as his grin produced a dimple in one cheek. That smile made her stomach do a funny flip.

"Alejandra, have you met my brother yet?" Anna's voice rose over the clatter of plates and forks.

Alejandra brought her head around to see who Anna was talking about. But Anna's smile was trained toward the cowboy. Señor Stewart. Edward. Her mind strained to understand what Anna meant, but it was like trying to run through deep water.

"I've had the pleasure of meeting Señorita Diaz." Señor Stewart's deep voice rumbled from across the table, pulling Alejandra's attention to his face. His mouth formed an amused tilt. "I'm glad to see you made it to our humble ranch."

Heat flamed up Alejandra's neck. He hadn't actually told the others they'd met before today. Should she say something about it? If she didn't, it would be like their own secret. Not that it was a bad secret. He'd saved her life, after all. Shouldn't they all know of his bravery?

But before she could speak, Anna said something to him in American. It sounded like she introduced him to Mama Sarita.

Señor O'Brien changed the conversation back to Spanish, as he addressed Mama Sarita and Alejandra. "Have you met the rest of the men? We've a good group of vaquero's on the Double Rocking B." He pointed to the man beside him. "This is Monty, our foreman. The place wouldn't run without him."

Monty dipped his chin in a sheepish grin. It was a nice smile, though, with his white teeth flashing against his tanned skin. He looked about Señor O'Brien's age, but a little more trail worn, perhaps.

"Then there's Miguel, and Juan." As his name was spoken, the old man who'd greeted them in the yard now grinned with a bob of his head. Señor O'Brien kept listing names as he pointed to each man around the table.

Alejandra offered a polite smile to each—almost all the men being her own countrymen—but she couldn't help darting glances out of the corner of her eye at the American across the table. And every time she did, he was watching her. It sent a flush of heat through her chest. What was it about this man that made her react so?

The conversation turned back to American, and Alejandra kept her eyes on her food while she tried to pick out words. They must be talking about the cattle. And something about cold. A river. Longhorns. Some of the words were close enough to the Spanish ones, she could understand if the person spoke slowly enough. She would get this. She had to.

After the men polished off the apple tamales, chairs scraped against the floor and boots thumped as the group rose. It had looked like there were a lot of people when they were all seated, but with so many men standing, their presence overpowered her small frame until there was hardly room to breathe. Alejandra slipped from her chair and into the kitchen. Whew.

Striding to the sink, she rolled up the sleeves of her best white shirtwaist. From the bar on the window sill, she scraped a few soap shavings into the bucket of wash water where the frying pans had been soaking.

"Alejandra?"

Whirling, she found Anna in the doorway, a friendly smile on her face and one hand settled on her middle. "Sí."

"Jacob thought you might like to walk out and see the horses with me and Emmaline. I haven't been out of the house all day." She brushed a hand over her wispy brown hair. "I could use some cool air."

Alejandra slipped her gaze from Anna to the near vacant dining room behind her. There was a table full of dishes to wash. No way could she leave with all this work to be done. But would it be rude to deny a request from their host?

Mama Sarita appeared in the doorway behind Anna, shifting her to the side with a gentle hand. "Alejandra." Her voice was stern. "My sister and I will take care of this washing. Go with Anna and let us work in peace."

With that command, Mama Sarita strode to Alejandra and pulled the cast iron pan from her hand. She dropped it into the water bucket with a "clunk." Then she propped a hand on each of Alejandra's shoulders, spun her toward the door, and pushed.

Alejandra fought to turn herself around so she could speak to the forceful woman. "Mama," she hissed. "I should stay in here to help. There's too much work to be done."

"Go with Anna." Mama Sarita had her at the door to the hall by now. With a firm pat on the back, she said, "Enjoy yourself," then spun back toward the kitchen and set to work.

A chuckle sounded from Anna as she stepped up to Alejandra and linked a hand through her elbow. "Let's go get some fresh air. I think these ladies want to work without us."

Emmaline scampered to meet them in the hallway, and Alejandra fought down her guilt while Anna helped her daughter with hat, coat, and mittens. Mama Sarita did deserve a chance to visit with her sister alone. After all, they'd been separated for all those years. If only she could have talked both women into letting her clean the table and kitchen, while they relaxed by the fire.

"All set?" Anna turned a cheery smile on Alejandra.

Squaring her shoulders, Alejandra grabbed her shawl from the peg, and stepped toward the door. "Let's go."

Anna frowned, not moving forward. "Do you have a warmer coat? The nights are getting cold."

Alejandra raised an arm to examine her wool shawl. Papa had brought home the strip of cloth as a gift, and she'd dyed it a deep red and embroidered blue forget-me-nots around the edges. It was one of her few luxuries. A special adornment that made her feel beautiful.

Anna examined the flowers in one corner. "This shawl is lovely, Alejandra. The needlework is amazing. Did you buy it in your hometown?"

"Sì. Papa bought the material, and I added the flowers."

Anna's gaze drifted over Alejandra, a new respect sparkling in her eyes. "You're so..." she paused, as if trying to think of the word in Spanish. "...talented."

Heat raced up Alejandra's neck, and her eyes fell to the shawl. "Gracias."

Anna slipped an arm around Alejandra's shoulders. "We'll need to make you a warmer coat, too. Texas winters can be awfully cold, with snow lasting for days or sometimes weeks. Jacob said he didn't think this winter would be as bad. But you'll still need something besides this lovely wrap."

She lifted a lantern from the wall as Emmaline led the way out onto the porch.

"Look, Mommy." The child spoke in a hushed tone, her face turned to the sky. "The moon's bigger tonight."

The mother and child discussed the night sky and the patterns of the moon as they walked. Alejandra lagged behind, staring up at all the twinkling lights against the black background. There were so many tonight, just like she used to see back home. The three stars of Orion's belt. The lion Leo.

They were all familiar. Like a comfortable blanket. So many things of this place reminded her of Mexico. The language the people spoke. The food. The stars overhead. Could it be, on this cattle ranch in the middle of Texas, she wasn't so very far from home?

After a pleasant quarter hour with Anna and Emmaline in the barn, Anna looped her hand around the crook in Alejandra's arm again and strolled toward the house. "You know, Alejandra. You're welcome to come ride any time. That Palomino mare is a good saddle horse. I can't go with you quite yet, but maybe Edward can, if he's in town. Or Jacob could send one of the hands out with you."

"Gracias." Alejandra's heart soared at the offer. A chance to ride again? The way she used to ride bareback through the dawn at Rancho Las Cuevas. But no. She had to rein in her daydreams. They lived in town, and it was a two hour wagon ride to this ranch. Her chances of riding at all were not likely, and certainly never in the first light of dawn.

When Emmaline pushed open the door to the house, Señor O'Brien met them in the hallway. "Would you ladies like to come into the den? We have some news to share."

News? Was it something private meant only for his wife and daughter? Perhaps she should go make herself useful in the kitchen. After all, she was the only one in the group who wasn't really family.

She was halfway down the hall when a deep voice called out. "Alejandra. Señorita Diaz."

His voice. It froze her feet, but sent her heart racing. Slowly, she swiveled in the direction from which it came.

There he stood. Edward. A sort of half-grin quirked one side of his mouth. "Won't you come hear the news?" He extended an elbow.

But she couldn't take her focus from his eyes. They spoke to her. Called her. Sent a warmth through her chest as if she were the most important person who existed in his life. How could a simple look say so much?

She found her feet moving of their own accord, carrying her to him. His gaze tracked her progress, never leaving her own. He slipped her hand into the crook of his arm, and guided her through the open door. His warmth radiated through the cloth of his sleeve, seeping through her body. She floated on air, walking next to this man.

A few gazes turned to them, and Alejandra noticed a twinkle in Anna's as she observed them. Edward escorted her to a wing-back chair, and Alejandra slipped into the soft cushion, heat finding its way to her face. She didn't quite have the nerve to meet his gaze with so many people around.

"It's been such a pleasure to have you ladies visit today." Señor O'Brien stood by the fireplace as he spoke in Spanish. Then with a warm smile at Tía Laura, who nestled on the couch next to Mama Sarita, he translated the words into American.

Scanning the rest of the group, he continued in Spanish. "It's not been healthy for my Anna to try to keep up with this house and cooking for the men, in her condition. Even with Emmaline here to help." He reached to tweak his daughter's nose as she snuggled next to her mother. She scrunched it in response, bringing a deep chuckle from him. This child was one of the cutest Alejandra had seen.

He addressed the group again. "So I'm very pleased to announce that Mama Sarita and Alejandra have agreed to join our little group, and share more of the cooking skills we sampled tonight." His gaze found first Mama Sarita, then Alejandra. "We look forward to your coming."

His words hit her like a blow to the head, leaving stars across her vision and a fuzziness in her mind. Join their group? What did that mean? A hand slipped around her shoulders, and Alejandra looked up into Mama Sarita's concerned face. The woman crouched down in front of Alejandra and leaned close to her ear so only Alejandra could hear the words.

"Mija, I'm sorry I didn't ask you first, but it sounded like the perfect solution. You've been concerned about finding a job, and the O'Briens need help. They're paying us good money, and we'll live here in the big house."

A paying job. Hadn't she hoped to find employment where she and Mama Sarita could work together as cooks or housekeepers? But she'd never quite envisioned this. Another ranch like Las Cuevas. Except the O'Briens, and even the vaqueros, seemed like good people. And then there was Edward. Did she want to be so near to him?

A groan pierced her thoughts as Anna pushed herself up from the chair next to Alejandra. Señor O'Brien was quick to reach out and help her, but Anna had one hand propped under her belly and another at her back. There was no way she could keep up with cooking and cleaning for the herd of vaqueros that had been in the dining room tonight. And caring for her daughter, too? Anna needed them. There was no doubt. And likely she'd need even more help when she had the babe.

She turned back to Mama Sarita, then released a long breath. "Sí. We'll stay and work here. It's good."

At least she hoped so.

Chapter Eight

THE next day, Alejandra perched on the wagon bench next to Mama Sarita and Tía Laura again, this time with all of their possessions folded into two bags in the bed behind them. The ride had grown long and silent. Surely they were nearing the ranch. At first, Mama Sarita tried to keep up cheerful conversation. But the knot in Alejandra's stomach silenced her. What if Alejandra couldn't keep them safe on this ranch? If something happened to Mama Sarita here, she could never forgive herself.

After a while, the three of them settled into melancholy silence. Out of the corner of her eye, she saw Tía Laura grasp Mama Sarita's hand. Was Tía Laura concerned for them? Or just sad to see her sister leave? What would it be like to have a sister? Not even decades apart could break such a strong bond. Would her own mother have given birth to another child if the French soldiers hadn't cut her life short?

Alejandra's fingers found their way to the scar on her cheek. That had been the worst day of her life. When the soldiers had ripped her from her mother's arms, she'd tried to fight back. They'd only laughed and hit Mama so hard she cried out. And then one of them pulled out that awful sword. She could still see the blood. Hear Mama's scream. More blood. Everywhere. Mama's blood. The burn on Alejandra's cheek as they'd tried to shut her up. *Mama!*

Alejandra bent over herself as a sob escaped. Why did it happen? How could God let the evil *soldados* murder her mother? A warm touch settled around Alejandra's shoulders. Mama?

Alejandra forced her eyes open. Mama Sarita. This woman had filled the void created that awful day. Alejandra leaned her head against Mama Sarita's shoulder, and drew in a deep breath.

By the time they pulled into the ranch yard at the Double Rocking B, Alejandra had composed herself. She nodded to the kind old man who helped them from the wagon. Was his name Juan? Yes, that sounded right.

Anna met them at the door with a bright smile. "I can't tell you how excited I am to have you here. Your company...not just the extra help." She quickly translated her words into American for Tía Laura, then beamed at her aunt's chuckle.

As soon as they'd hung their cloaks on the pegs in the hall, Anna turned and motioned for them to follow her. "Emmaline's taking an early nap, so the house is quiet right now. I'll wait till she's up before I show you to your rooms, if you don't mind. I'm heating your chicken tortilla soup from yesterday for lunch. It was *sooo* good. I thought you might like something warm after riding for hours in the cold. The men are working in the North pasture again today so they won't be back until tonight."

She paused her chatter long enough to turn and throw a grin at them. "It was handy to have the leftover tamales to send out with them for lunch. You're both so clever. Have I told you how thankful I am you've agreed to come stay with us?"

Alejandra bit back a smile. Maybe this would be good for them all.

Emmaline woke up while they ate, and stumbled into the dining room with hair rumpled and a cloth doll tucked under one arm. She stopped and took in the sight of the women sitting around the table, her sleepy gaze ignoring their greetings. She charged forward, and headed straight for…Alejandra. Before Alejandra knew what was happening, the child climbed onto her lap. Her hands instinctively wrapped around the little girl, and snuggled her close.

"I think she's found a friend." Anna placed another bowl of soup in front of them.

Alejandra soaked in the little girl smell while Emmaline ate. There couldn't be anything better than the love of a child.

Alejandra could have sat and snuggled with Emmaline all day, but Tía Laura rose and began stacking dishes to carry to the kitchen. Emmaline slid from Alejandra's lap to help her aunt.

Tía Laura spoke to Anna, something about "rooms," "Emmy," and "bowls." Anna nodded and motioned for Mama Sarita and Alejandra to follow her. "Come, I'll show you to your rooms."

Elaborate railing lined the staircase, carved from the richest cherry Alejandra had ever seen. A layer of dust filled the crevices of the carving, but with a little polishing, no doubt the color would come to life.

At the top of the stairs, Anna turned right and opened the first door she came to, leaning against it as she paused to catch her breath. It must be hard to climb so many steps carrying so much extra weight in her middle. "I thought Mama Sarita might like this room. It belonged to Jacob's Aunt Lola for many years." Anna's voice seemed to catch at the memory. "She helped raise him and was my dearest friend when I first came to the ranch. It's been hard since we lost her last year." Her voice dropped to a whisper at the end.

A strong urge welled in Alejandra's chest to reach out and touch the other woman. Lay an understanding hand on her shoulder. She knew what it was like to lose a dear friend. But would that be appropriate toward her employer?

Before she could make up her mind, Anna turned to face Alejandra, a forced smile coming through the tears in her eyes. Anna reached a hand to Alejandra's back, the same way Alejandra had almost done to her. "You know what it means to lose a good friend, too. It's such a comfort to have you both here."

How had she done it? Not only had Anna set aside the boundaries of being an employer and made Alejandra feel like a friend, she'd put into words exactly what Alejandra wanted to express.

Moisture clouded her own eyes as she stared at this kind American woman. All she could manage to choke out was, "Sí." But she could see it in Anna's eyes. She understood.

When Anna led her to the next door and motioned for her to step inside, Alejandra sucked in a breath at the sight before her. This wasn't what she'd expected.

The large, sturdy pine bed dominated the middle of the room. Its exquisite quilt had a star design, pieced together from red like the stain of blackberries, forest green, and blue as vibrant as a bluebird.

"Oh," she breathed, stepping forward to caress the soft fabric. A flash of color in the corner of her vision brought Alejandra's attention to the windows, where curtains of the same rich red material hung from the twin windows on either side of the bed. An arm chair rested under the glass on the left, and a pine bureau and mirror to match sat in the opposite corner. The room breathed an aura of comfortable luxury.

"This is the chamber I stayed in when Jacob's father first hired me to cook for the ranch. I loved it then." A smile touched her voice. "I haven't brought myself to change anything. Not even the quilt."

"It's perfect." Alejandra spun to face Anna, moisture stinging her eyes again. "Thank you, Señora O'Brien. You've given so much to Mama Sarita and me. I hope one day we'll be able to repay you."

Anna stepped forward and pulled Alejandra into a hug. A real hug, although the fullness in her midsection kept them apart. When Anna leaned back, the moisture in her eyes matched that in Alejandra's. "The only thing I want from you, Alejandra Diaz, is the gift of your friendship. And I will treasure it always."

ONCE they'd settled in, Alejandra helped Mama Sarita with the evening meal. Anna sat in a kitchen chair, and Emmaline snuggled her doll in a miniature quilt.

"It's time for my baby to sleep now," the little angel said in a high, make-believe tone. She started a soft humming, and rocked the little bundle with enough force to make the cloth baby seasick.

"Are you sure I can't help with anything?" Anna asked for the third time. If it weren't for the exhaustion evident in the dark hollows under her eyes, Alejandra would have been tempted to let her chop peppers just to feel useful. But Anna needed to rest.

"The food is under control." Mama Sarita spoke up, her tone patient and reassuring. "But you can help by telling us how the ranch runs. I did not see rooms for the vaqueros in the main house, no? They sleep in one of the other buildings?"

Anna nodded. "Yes, Jacob built onto the bunkhouse last year. All the men sleep out there except Edward, when he's home. When he's here, he sleeps in Jacob's old room upstairs at the other end of the hall. He'll be leaving for another assignment tomorrow, though." Anna's voice tightened.

Edward slept in the main house? But, of course he would. Still, that would put him just down the hall from her. And what had Anna meant by an assignment? Could she ask? No. She was here to work, not learn more about that handsome cowboy. "We'll need to clean the bunkhouse, too, sí?"

"No." Anna shook her head. "Monty runs a tight ship and makes the men clean up after themselves. Even makes them do laundry every week. I go in and do a thorough cleaning in the spring and fall, but otherwise I stay out of the bunkhouse." She shrugged. "I know it's hard to believe, but it stays neater than the big house at times."

She leaned forward and tugged on Emmaline's braid. "Certainly cleaner than this one's bedroom."

Emmaline touched a finger to her lips and spoke in a loud whisper, "Shhh. Clara's sleeping."

IT'S a good thing Alejandra and Mama Sarita worked together for the evening meal, because they barely had all the food ready in time. It was the twelfth of December, Día de Nuestra Señora de Guadalupe—the day to honor Our Lady of Guadalupe. For the celebration, they'd prepared some of the traditional feast recipes.

As she carried the tray of buñuelos, Alejandra inhaled the unique aroma of cinnamon and anise. Of all the smells that took her back to happier days in her childhood, this was her favorite. The simple balls of yeast dough were easy enough to make, then fry, and smother in sweet cinnamon sauce.

The vaqueros probably hadn't tasted any in quite a while, and maybe never any as good as the recipe her madre passed down. She wasn't able to find any canned guava on Anna's shelves, so she used apples instead for the sauce. Hopefully, the taste would still be good.

Regardless of the outcome of the buñuelo sauce, tonight they would celebrate.

Men trickled into the dining room as she placed the platter on the table. Alejandra stepped back to examine the expanse of overflowing serving dishes and utensils. Were they missing anything? The whipped sour cream was there. Tortillas. Rice. Chicken marinating in its spicy tomato sauce. Tortas, another festival favorite. Everything seemed to be in place.

"Come and sit now, mija," Mama Sarita whispered from behind. "The dinner is perfect."

Alejandra obeyed as the rest of the group settled into chairs. Her gaze strayed toward the seat Edward had occupied yesterday, but it stood empty. Was he out with the herd still? Anna had said something about an "assignment," but hadn't she said that was tomorrow? His absence shouldn't create this pit of disappointment in her, should it?

After Señor O'Brien spoke the prayer, the men scooped food onto their plates and dove into the fare with abandon. Alejandra could only stare as they devoured what had taken her and Mama Sarita all afternoon to make. Had they never eaten good food before? Or was this the way they always consumed their meals? Could they even taste the rich flavor of the cuaresmeño peppers in the sauce?

Conversation was minimal as the sounds of fork against plate overtook everything else. The old man called Juan was the first to speak. "This feels like a fiesta, sí?" His dark eyes twinkled.

Mama Sarita answered, "It's a celebration day, is it not? Día de Nuestra Señora de Guadalupe."

Juan formed the sign of the cross upon his chest. "Señora de Guadalupe. She is our country's symbol for everything that is good. I'm honored to live by the river called by her name."

What? A river named for the Virgin Guadalupe? "What river, Señor?"

Anna interjected an enthusiastic answer before Juan had a chance. "Oh, you have to see the Guadalupe River, Alejandra. There's a beautiful spot that borders our land to the northeast. If I could, I'd take you out there tomorrow. Or maybe we could ride in the buggy..." She looked to her husband as she spoke, and her voice trailed off when he shook his head vehemently.

Turning a weak smile back to Alejandra, she continued. "Or maybe one of the cowboys can show you." And then her face brightened like a sun's ray. "Edward. I'll ask Edward to take you to the river the next time he's here for the day. He had to ride into Seguin this afternoon, and then he'll leave for an assignment tomorrow morning. But he should be back in a few days."

So that's why Edward's chair was empty. Dare she ask what an assignment was? It sounded like he'd be leaving town for it. Maybe she could question Anna later when there weren't so many ears around.

"I'll never forget the time our family traveled to the Villa de Guadalupe Hidalgo to celebrate the Virgin Guadalupe's appearance all those years ago. The festival was amazing." Juan held up one of the fried bread balls from his plate. "And the buñuelos were my favorite. But not so good as this." To prove his point, he popped the round sweet in his mouth, his face scrunching into a look of pure pleasure.

Alejandra bit back a smile, as warmth flooded her chest. These people showed such appreciation and emotion. She'd never seen anything quite like it.

Would Edward do the same?

Chapter Nine

ALEJANDRA shuffled around the table the next morning, setting a white ironstone plate at each chair. The dishes were beautiful, with wide fluted edges and delicate leaf prints pressed into the sides. She'd never used anything so lovely. And to put them out for the vaqueros to eat from? It seemed *loco*.

"If that food tastes as good as it smells, I'm sorry I have to miss it."

The deep male voice resonated across the room, sending Alejandra at least three inches off the floor. Her heart stopped for a split second, then thundered in her chest. "What in the world?" She spun toward the voice.

There stood Edward Stewart. He was halfway across the room, but even from this distance she could see his mouth quirked, exposing one of his dimples. "Sorry if I startled you." He held up a cloth sack. "Just came by to pack some food before I head out."

Head out? Alejandra blinked to clear her mind. He was leaving already? She pushed herself into action. Striding forward, she reached to take the sack from him. "I'll pack lunch for you. Will you stay for breakfast before you go?"

She was close enough now to touch him, and warmth crept up her neck at his nearness. She couldn't look at his face, so she kept her gaze on the sack as he handed it to her. He wore a gun today, like that day he'd saved her in San Antonio. But had he worn it the other day when they first visited the ranch? Not that she remembered. It was probably a good idea for him to be armed when he traveled, though.

"Afraid I don't have time to eat here. I'll just snack on the trail."

With the cloth sack in her hand, she spun toward the kitchen. "I'll fill this and be right back." She scurried through the doorway, conscious of the boot thuds that followed at a slower pace.

"Buenas dias, Señora." His voice was warm as he greeted Mama Sarita, who stood at the stove tossing corn tortillas in a pan.

Mama Sarita kept up a lively chatter with him while Alejandra focused on filling his pack. There were a few tamales left from the other night. She wrapped the apple one in a separate cloth. Tortillas. A hunk of cheese. A generous bundle of buñuelos. Too bad she didn't have a way to wrap the arroz con pollo. How long would he be gone exactly? She turned to ask him…

And froze.

What was that on his chest? Something metal glimmered in the light from the window. A star? Her chest burned, and she struggled to breathe.

A badge? Edward wore a badge? *No!* He couldn't be a soldier. Could he? But only soldiers wore badges.

He must have noticed the stricken look on her face, because he stopped in the middle of speaking to Mama Sarita. His brows lowered. "What's wrong?"

Alejandra spun away from him. What was wrong? Everything! How could they be living in the home of a soldier? The kind that killed Mama. And Papa. How could she let this happen?

And how could it be Edward? She bit down hard on her lower lip to hold a sob inside.

An ache in her fingers penetrated Alejandra's awareness. She looked down, and found her knuckles white as they gripped the satchel. She had to get him out of here. Her body vaulted into motion, stuffing all the food she'd laid out on the counter into the satchel. No matter what the items were. She didn't care anymore. All she wanted was for him to leave.

Pulling the drawstring tight on the bag, she whirled and shoved it at him. "Here."

She didn't miss the shock on his face as he reflexively clutched the bundle. But she ignored it. Spinning back to the work counter, she busied herself laying out serving dishes to use for breakfast. She wouldn't leave the room until he was gone. Couldn't leave a soldier alone with Mama Sarita.

The room grew silent, but for the clanging of the dishes as she dropped them on the counter. Had he left already? But then came a shuffle, and the tell-tale sound of boots thudding on the hard wooden floor. The steps grew quieter as he retreated down the hall, then disappeared in the sound of the closing door.

WHAT had just happened? Edward paused on the front porch to replay the last few minutes in his mind. One moment Alejandra was giving him one of her shy smiles, and the next she looked at him as if he were a two-headed demon. Had he done something to anger or upset her? Not that he could remember. Certainly not anything he'd intended to do.

Mama Sarita was telling him what Emmaline had said about her "favorite Uncle Eddie." That shouldn't have upset Alejandra. So what then? He wasn't dumb enough to think she was upset about him leaving, even if he wanted that to be the case.

A horse nickered from the corral beside the barn, pulling Edward's gaze in that direction. He had to get going if he was going to make it to Austin in time to meet the other Texas Rangers. With a weight in his chest, he turned and strode down the steps.

For the first time in two years, he hated leaving the ranch. Especially without knowing what had upset Alejandra.

"MIJA."

Alejandra didn't look up from the peppers she chopped, but the concern—and hint of reprimand—in Mama Sarita's voice was hard to miss.

"The huevos rancheros are better with chunks of peppers, not powder."

Powder? She paused for a glance at the green vegetable scattered under her knife. It wasn't powder, but the pieces were somewhat shredded. Or mutilated might be a better word.

A gentle hand touched her shoulder. "Mija, what's wrong?"

Without warning, tears blurred her vision, their sting a perfect match to the burning in her chest. A sob escaped, and she clamped a hand over her mouth, just as Mama pulled her into an embrace. The tears would no longer be held back. Standing there in the kitchen, with Mama Sarita holding her close...she wept.

At last she pulled back, and with a shuddering breath, wiped her eyes with her apron.

"Now, mija. Can you tell me what happened this morning?" Mama Sarita's eyes held only concern as she studied Alejandra.

Alejandra's gaze skittered down to where her fingers wrapped around her apron hem. She had to tell Mama Sarita. Right? So the older woman would be wary? Or maybe they should leave the ranch. Yes. They had to leave.

She looked up to meet Mama Sarita's gaze. "The badge. He's a *soldado*, Mama Sarita. He wore the badge of a soldado." She gripped the older woman's arm. "We must leave here. We can't stay in the same house with him." Panic sounded in her voice, and she watched for that same emotion to appear on Mama Sarita's face.

But it was sadness that flickered there. The woman opened her mouth to speak, then paused, uncertainty wrinkling her forehead. "Alejandra. Señor Stewart is a good man. He's Anna's brother. A *good* soldier."

A good soldier? There wasn't such a thing. "We have to leave."

"No, mija." Mama Sarita's voice held a quiet firmness.

"But…"

Mama Sarita laid a hand on her forearm. "This is where God has planted us. We're needed here. We'll stay." And with that, she turned back to the work counter and began cracking eggs into a bowl.

So many emotions swirled in Alejandra's chest, she couldn't think straight. Just like that, they were staying here?

Under the same roof as a soldado? Mama Sarita said he was a good soldier, but that wasn't possible.

All soldiers killed.

"QUIT yer squirmin', Jack. Won't do any good." Edward eyed the man who sat atop the horse beside him. "Slope-back Jack," as he was known to the general public, twisted his upper body in an effort to get at the rope that bound his hands. The man could wind himself up like a knotted yarn if he wanted, but that rope was tied tight, in so many knots a sailor would be proud.

Jack snarled, the ugly pink scar beside his eye not hidden by the scruffy growth on his face. As scars went, that was a nasty one. Must not have had any medical care when the wound happened.

Edward's mind drifted to a scar on another face. Had Alejandra seen a doctor for the scar that edged her cheek? Hers was only a pink line, stretching from the point of her beautiful cheekbone to her cute little ear. What had caused it? An accident on the ranch she lived on before she left Mexico?

He'd pried enough from Anna to know Alejandra and her father worked on a large ranch there, until he died recently. But Anna wouldn't say more, even though she rarely kept secrets from him. When he'd pushed, her face took on a serious expression, and she said he'd have to learn the rest from

Alejandra. What did that mean? It must be bad, whatever had happened.

Did it have anything to do with the way Alejandra had looked at him the morning he left on this assignment?

A sudden thought flashed in his mind. An awful thought. Had someone hurt her? Maybe something that happened in the kitchen that morning had brought back a terrible memory. His chest tied in knots like the ones holding the prisoner captive. What terrible thing had Alejandra suffered? If it had to do with her scar, it couldn't have been very recent.

His horse bobbed its head, jerking at the reins. Oops. He'd been squeezing with his legs at the same time his hands had a stranglehold on the reins. Poor animal, getting conflicting signals from him. Relaxing both his legs and the reins, he reached down to pat the gelding. "Sorry, boy."

But if he ever got his hands on the louse that hurt Alejandra, Edward wouldn't be sorry.

The man would pay. Dearly.

THE next day, apprehension tightened Edward's chest as he rode into the yard of the Double Rocking B. He'd been more eager to come home after this assignment than any he'd had yet, but would Alejandra be back to her normal self? Would she flash that timid smile at him when he told her how good the food was she'd packed for him? That smile could make a man hike barefoot through a cactus grove.

Juan stepped from the barn and shuffled toward Edward as he dismounted.

"Hello, boss." The older cowhand still spoke with a heavy Mexican accent. Juan had been on the ranch before Edward and Anna came, and he was getting up in years now. Not so much that he didn't want to feel useful, but riding herd all day took too much toll on his weather beaten body. Taking care of the barns and stock around the house seemed a good fit for the dedicated cowpuncher now. Besides, it was nice to have a man close to the house to protect the women. Just in case.

"Amigo." Edward extended a hand and a smile to greet the man.

"I take your horse. Give him a good rub down and corn."

"No, Juan. I can take care of Pepper." A decent cowboy always took care of his horse. That's the first thing Monty taught him about riding with the cowpunchers as a lanky fifteen-year-old.

But Juan didn't seem to have any intention of obeying orders. He grabbed Pepper's reins and started toward the barn. "I bring your bedroll in later. If you hurry, you'll be in time for the lunch," he called over his shoulder.

Shaking his head, Edward removed his hat and slapped it against his leg as he turned toward the front door. Would Alejandra be as eager to see him as he was to feast his eyes on her?

A savory aroma with a hint of spice greeted him when he stepped through the front door. Women's voices drifted down the hallway, and he followed them into the dining room. Anna, Mama Sarita, and Alejandra ate at the far end of the table. Conversation stopped when they saw him, and Mama Sarita rose quickly and strode to the kitchen.

"Sit down, Señor Stewart. I'll bring your plate out."

His normal seat was in the middle of the table, but it didn't seem right to leave so much space between him and the ladies. So he sat in the first empty seat near them. Just around the table's corner from Alejandra.

She hadn't looked at him yet, but he couldn't stop staring at her. Her sleek black hair was wrapped in a knot at the back of her neck, and stray wisps framed her face. Each of her features was so refined, almost like a china doll. She was breathtaking. Truly.

But she steadfastly ignored him.

Mama Sarita shuffled from the kitchen with a bowl in one hand and a small plate in the other. Steam wafted from the bowl, along with that same aroma he'd noticed when he first entered the house.

"Mmmm... Chili and Bean soup?" He raised a questioning gaze to the older woman.

The skin around her eyes creased into a cheery smile. "Sí. And Anna made the cornbread for tonight's dinner. You will have an early taste."

He shot a grin at his sister. "Yep, Anna makes the best spicy cornbread in Texas."

"You haven't tried Alejandra's yet," Anna shot back. "She made it for us two nights ago, and it makes mine taste like I forgot to add the water."

"Really?" Edward paused from eating to watch Alejandra's reaction to the compliment. She sent Anna a quick smile that didn't reach her dark eyes, then dropped her focus back to the brown mixture in her bowl.

"I can't wait til you make it again." He tried to keep his voice gentle.

She made no visible reaction to his words, except for a slight stiffening of her spine. And then he saw white knuckles where she held the spoon. If she squeezed any harder, that poor metal spoon would bend in half.

What was wrong with her? Was she this tense all the time? Or just when he was around? But she hadn't seemed to be uptight or reserved before. Maybe a bit in San Antonio after he scared off those thugs. But even then, when she hadn't known him from Methuselah, she'd been more relaxed and affable than she was now.

As soon as the meal ended, Alejandra darted to the kitchen and didn't reappear. It was high time he figured out what was going on.

Chapter Ten

EDWARD ran a hand through his hair. Maybe he should clean himself up before tracking down Alejandra. At the very least, change shirts and dunk his head in a bowl of water to rinse the sweat off. And maybe a quick shave. Too bad he hadn't stopped for a haircut on his way through Seguin.

A half hour later, he was as clean as he could get without a barber and a bathtub. Jogging down the stairs, he fingered the cut on his right cheek where he'd gotten sidetracked with the razor.

Voices and laughter drifted from the kitchen, so he headed there first. Emmaline and Mama Sarita sat at the small round table, the little girl giggling at something the woman said. Alejandra was nowhere in sight.

Emmaline turned that little cherub face on him. "Uncle Eddie, Mama Sarita's telling me about the three piggies."

He tweaked her chin. "One of my favorites." Turning to the older woman, he asked, "Is Alejandra around? I need to ask her a question."

Her face took on a sad half-smile. "She's in the back, doing the washing."

Nodding, he turned toward the door that led from the kitchen to the rear yard. A blast of cold hit him as he stepped outside. Maybe he should get his coat first. But then he saw Alejandra, and all other thoughts disappeared. She wore what looked like one of Anna's old cloaks, the brown color sharing the same dreary feel of the leafless trees lining the clearing. Even the rose bushes Jacob had planted for Anna beside the house had lost their green leaves and yellow blooms. They now stood as sad skeletons huddled against the chill.

Alejandra's back faced him as she bent over the wash tub, scrubbing. He made a wide arc so he approached her from the side. The last thing he wanted to do was startle her, and add that offense on top of whatever else had her so upset.

He stopped a length away from her. "Alejandra?" He cringed at the hesitation in his voice.

She didn't react. Just kept scrubbing at a piece of red flannel.

He tried again, in slow Spanish, this time making sure his voice carried a little more strength. "Is something wrong? Have I upset you?"

Nothing. Not even a stiffening of her shoulders.

"I want to help. Please. You can trust me."

That got a reaction. Like a sleeping bear waking, she straightened up from the washtub, and shot him a look that could have boiled water in a snowstorm. He took a step back before he realized his action.

"Trust you?" Her eyes sparked, like a red hot horseshoe pulled from a forge. She rattled off a string of rapid-fire Spanish that took all his focus to try to understand. Only one word clearly stood out to him. Probably because she spit it with the vehemence of a cornered mountain lion.

Soldado.

And with that word, she flung the red flannel back into the wash bucket, whirled, and fled into the house. The door banged shut behind her.

Soldado? Soldier?

What did she mean by that? Edward shook his head to clear it. This wasn't making a bit of sense.

Was there something in her Mexican background that made her hate soldiers? But how could he know what? Who could he ask? Maybe Mama Sarita would share some of Alejandra's history. But would she really share such details about her beloved friend? Not even his own sister would open up to him.

And then a face popped into his mind. Monty. Monty had lived in Mexico. He wouldn't know anything specific about Alejandra, but maybe he'd know what Mexicans might have against soldiers in general. Or what that had to do with him. And besides, Monty was about the wisest man Edward had ever known. It was uncanny, the knowledge he held.

Edward saddled an Appaloosa gelding and set off toward the North pastures where Anna said the cattle grazed. He finally found the herds in the farthest section, near the line shack where the cowboys took turns staying when the weather got bad.

Monty sat on his horse near the edge of the tree line, still as an oak tree while he stared at the animals. As Edward neared, Monty didn't turn, but his lips moved as if he counted something. The cattle?

Edward halted his horse next to Monty's. And waited. His friend would speak when he was ready. Until then, he'd do best to let the man alone.

As he waited, Edward took in the sight before him. A cool breeze wafted over him, bringing with it the familiar scent of cattle and dust, and the occasional snorts and sounds of tearing grass as the cattle grazed. There was nothing quite like working with a herd of cattle. It got down deep in the soul of a man. Took away the stress and strain of dealing with people. Just you and the animals and the elements.

"You come to work?" Monty's voice finally broke the peaceful spell.

Edward glanced over, but the man wasn't looking at him. He still faced the cattle, but one side of his mouth held a slight tilt. "I'm at your disposal, boss."

Now both sides of Monty's mouth tipped. And it was clear he was fighting the grin that showed in his eyes. "Fancy lawman like you shouldn't be out punchin' cattle with the likes of us."

Coming from any other man, that might have been a jab. But Monty knew Edward had enjoyed his eight years working as a cow hand on Jacob and Anna's ranch. And he knew better than any other how much Edward craved independence. And respect. To be more than just Anna's "Little Brother." And as a Texas Ranger, he'd succeeded.

They settled into silence again. How should he go about questioning Monty? Just come out and ask if there's any reason a Mexican woman would be afraid of soldiers? The approach seemed a bit direct. Soldiers were supposed to be good people. He didn't want to insult the man's country by insinuating the lawmen there were scoundrels. Nope, dancin' around the fencepost was the way to go here.

"Monty, when someone says *soldados*, are they talking about actual soldiers, or just lawmen in general?"

Monty raised a brow, but didn't turn it on Edward. "That's usually talkin' specific about soldiers." It was amazing how Monty had dropped most of his Mexican accent, and picked up the southern twang of most of the local Seguinites.

"So...are there a lot of soldiers in Mexico?" He kept his tone casual.

"Depends on where you're talkin'. And when." Monty's horse shifted its weight from one back leg to another. "Up around the border, near Tamaulipas where the pretty Señorita and your aunt's sister are from, I don't think there's many actual soldiers there these days. Just a bunch of informal militia. Course back about ten years ago, when the French took it over, the place was swarmin' with 'em. *Soldados Franceses* everywhere. They were a rough lot, from what I hear. I'd left Mexico just before they came, though, so can't say for sure."

French soldiers? Ten years was a while ago. But if the episode had been frightening enough, it could leave scars on a person's mind. Especially a young girl's. *Scars.* Is that where the scar on Alejandra's cheek came from? It looked like it could be about ten years old. Definitely not recent.

Horns and handguns. No wonder she spat the word *soldados* like she might tear him apart with her bare hands. But why exactly did she think he was a soldier? Had he ever actually told Alejandra what he did for a living? A Texas Ranger was a far cry from a soldier. They didn't even wear uniforms, just dressed like a cowpuncher. He did wear a badge for most of his assignments, though. Could that be the connection for her?

"Monty, you have any idea if the French soldiers wore uniforms? Or maybe some kind of badge?"

Monty squinted, his face taking on that faraway, calculating look again. "Seems to me they did. Always wore gray jackets with gold buttons parading down the front, and some kind of gold badge sewn over the heart."

A rock settled in Edward's stomach, weighing him down. Did Alejandra think he was a soldier because he wore a badge? Is that why she changed so suddenly when she saw his badge three days ago? But surely she'd seen it before. He thought back to the first time they met in San Antonio. He'd been on his way to an assignment then. But it had been undercover, so he'd left his badge off. The rock in his stomach threatened to rise with the bile climbing into his throat.

God, what do I do? Alejandra thought he was a soldier? Thought he was as evil as whoever had hurt her all those years ago? His nails dug into his palms as his hands clenched.

"Patience, amigo. It's going to take lots of persistence to prove you're different."

Edward jerked his head to look at Monty. "What are you talking about?"

Monty's mouth twitched. "To show that pretty Señorita you're a good soldier. And if her past is as bad as you think it is, she may not ever trust you."

The man was too good at reading minds. That's probably why he could outsmart even the cleverest longhorns.

Edward turned back to the sea of brown and black hides stretched across the pasture before them. "Patience and persistence, huh. Anything else?"

"Not unless you plan to turn in your badge."

Turn in his badge? Not likely.

ALEJANDRA bent low over the soft cotton cloth as she threaded her smocking needle through the layers. "So do you have names picked out for a boy and girl?"

Anna's lips pinched as she rolled her eyes. "We've had a boy's name picked out since before Emmaline was born. Martin Timothy, after both our pas. But girl's names seem to be a problem. We had trouble agreeing on Emmy's name, and can't agree on a girl's name this time, either." A smile touched her mouth as her gaze dropped back to the gown she stitched. "I think I'm just going to hold out until she's born and hope Jacob's so overwhelmed by the birth he gives in."

A giggle rose before Alejandra could hold it back. "You two are quite a pair. Although, the way Señor O'Brien looks at you, I can't believe he'd deny you anything."

They settled into an easy silence, which Anna finally broke with a soft chuckle. "My sewing was so bad when I was a girl. Until Mama died and I had to do the mending. I patched so many holes in Edward's clothes, my stitches became the smallest among the women in our circle. And Edward didn't just get holes in the elbows and knees of his clothes. He would get big tears in the strangest places—along the sides, the backs, the shoulders. I mended and patched them all." Her mouth pulled into a rueful smile. "And he was always growing. I let out more hems than I could count."

An image of a lanky, brown-haired boy flitted into Alejandra's mind, squeezing something in her chest. She had to stop thinking about him. Latching onto the only part of Anna's comment that didn't pertain to Edward, she asked, "How old were you when your mama died?"

A deep sigh drifted from Anna.

Oh, no. What had she been thinking to ask about such a distressing topic? "I'm sorry. I…"

But Anna shook her head. "No, I don't mind you asking. I was eleven when Mama died. It was hard. Really hard. I lost her just when I was trying to learn to be a young lady. Then having to teach myself how to run a household and take care of Papa and Edward." She breathed another sigh. "I wouldn't have made it through without God's help." Glancing at Alejandra, she added. "But I guess you know what I mean, don't you? How old were you when your mama passed away?"

Alejandra inhaled a deep breath, willing down the anger that always surfaced when she thought of Mama's death. "I was twelve. And yes, it was hard." She tried for a carefree chuckle, but it came out sounding more bitter than anything. "But I had to do it myself. I didn't have God to help."

Anna's eyes shone in a sad smile. "He was there, Alejandra. I promise. Even when it didn't feel like it."

Anger welled up in Alejandra like boiling water. "He was there? When the soldiers ripped my mama from me and slashed her with a sword? If he was there, why didn't he stop them from murdering her, while I was forced to watch? They took away the madre who gave life to me, and left me with only this scar to remember her by." Her fingers found the mark on her face, and the touch brought back the searing pain of sharp metal ripping her flesh.

But then warm skin touched her hand, resting across her fingers that covered the scar.

"Alejandra, you may not be ready to hear what I'm about to say. But tuck these words away, and pull them out again later, as your heart needs them. Sometimes things happen that don't make sense, and it's hard to believe God can love us and still let those things happen. But God has a plan. His plan for your mother was to take her to a better place. And His plan for you is to give you a hope and a future."

She settled her other hand on Alejandra's bare cheek, framing her face between both palms. "But, Alejandra, moving forward into that future requires forgiving God for the past."

The burn of tears threatened to choke out her self-control. She had to restrain them. Couldn't let herself dwell on Anna's words now. That would be the end of her.

Drawing a deep, shuddering breath, Alejandra pulled back. Away from Anna's gentle touch that just might be her undoing. She flicked the back of a finger under her eye where a single tear had escaped her barrier. Then she took up the tiny gown in one hand, and her smocking needle in the other. She couldn't meet Anna's eyes. Couldn't face the disappointment she was bound to see.

Silence stretched between them again, as Anna resumed her sewing, too. But the quiet was torture. Too many memories fought for attention. She couldn't let them surface, or she would lose control. Clearing her throat, Alejandra searched for a new conversation topic. One that would surely be safe. "Would you like me to put out your nativity scene? Since today is Las Posadas?"

Anna's brows almost met as her forehead wrinkled. "Las Posadas? What does that mean?"

"It's the celebration when we set out the nativity. Then Papa would lead our friends in a parade to the scene. The same way Joseph and Mary searched for the inn."

A light filled Anna's eyes. "What a great idea." But her mouth pinched. "Unfortunately, we don't have a crèche. But I'll make sure Jacob remedies that before next year."

They didn't have a nativity set? "Do you...celebrate Navidad?"

Anna blinked. "Christmas? Oh, yes. That's one of my favorite holidays. It might be simpler this year, because of my...condition." She motioned toward her expanded middle.

Alejandra sat straighter. "But that's why we're here. Tell me what you normally do, and I'll make sure it's taken care of." Finally, she'd be able to really make a difference.

A smile spread across Anna's mouth. "Okay, then. I guess we should talk about the Christmas dinner first."

Chapter Eleven

THE day before Navidad—or Christmas as the Americans called it—a special mood seemed to fill the air. A sense of anticipation. It shimmered in the eyes of the vaqueros as they sat around the breakfast table. The spark even shone in Edward's eyes. Until she shot him a hard glare. That snuffed it out quickly enough. It still didn't seem fathomable that a woman as kind and sweet as Anna could have a brother who was a soldier.

As soon as the men left the house and the breakfast dishes were cleared, Anna brought out a huge bowl that had been tucked in the storage closet. She uncovered it for the women to see. "I thought we could string some popped corn for the Christmas tree."

Emmaline clapped her hands. "Goodie!"

They settled into chairs around the fire in the living room, and with the group of them working, had several strings of popped corn assembled in no time. Although, Alejandra still

105

wasn't quite sure what they would do with it now that the strings were complete.

The front door opened, and the sounds of scraping and shuffling echoed from the hall. "Did someone ask for a Christmas tree?" a male voice called.

"Papa!" Emmaline squealed, jumping up from her perch on the floor and leaping toward the hall.

A man appeared in the doorway, his broad shoulders not disguised under the wool coat. Edward. Her stomach did a flutter before she squashed the feeling. He carried something as he shuffled backward. Something big and bushy.

A tree. Alejandra stared at the man-sized pine tree Edward and Señor O'Brien hauled into the room and leaned against a wall in the corner. When Anna talked about a Christmas tree, she'd thought it would be some kind of decorated evergreen clippings or maybe even a waist-high shrub. Not this massive tree. They'd need to string popped corn all day to have any hope of making the strands wrap around these branches more than twice.

Emmaline danced around the men as they worked to secure it in a wood platform Señor O'Brien brought in. "May I string the corn now? Please?"

Edward chuckled, the rich sound rising from his chest. "All right, Emmie-bug. Bring a rope of it over."

The child scooped an armful and carried it to the tree, plopping it on the floor. "Where do we start?"

"Well." He squatted beside the girl. "The first thing every cowgirl needs to learn is how to take care of her equipment." He picked up the popcorn string at one end, and began looping it loosely over his hand. "You have to keep your lasso from getting tangled up. See?"

He was so gentle with the child. Holding the loop and following her around while she placed it just so on the tree. How could this man be a soldier who murdered people and tore apart families? It didn't make sense.

After the tree was garnished, Anna called for Emmaline to take her daily nap.

"Mama, can I please stay up and watch the tree a while longer?" The little girl turned those pleading blue eyes on her mother. How in the world could Anna say no? But one look at her friend showed a resolute expression that wouldn't allow her mind to be changed.

Alejandra stepped forward and scooped up Emmaline's hand. "Come, niña. I'll tell you a story about my favorite Navidad before you go to sleep?"

Emmaline gripped Alejandra's hand with her soft chubby one as they left the room and headed up the stairs. The trust in that action started a longing in Alejandra's chest. How wonderful it was to have a child to love.

ALEJANDRA settled back in her chair and eyed the activity as their big Christmas meal dwindled to a close. It looked to have been a success, if the empty plates and dishes strewn across the mahogany wood surface was any indication. The food had been a challenge, for sure. The tamales and roasted turkey were familiar, but Anna also taught her how to make mashed potatoes, and a thick gray substance she called gravy. And then there was the apple pie, with a filling not unlike a sweet tamale, but the outside was so different from the corn batter. But, oh, she could still taste the amazing flavor on her tongue.

At least a few of the vaqueros seemed to like it, too. As she watched, Miguel reached for the pie tin that had only a single piece left. But Donato was too quick for him, grabbing the pan and almost dumping the sweet onto his plate.

"Hey." Miguel frowned, like a child who'd had his favorite toy taken away. Then a glimmer touched his eye, and he reached to scoop a forkful of pie from Donato's plate.

Donato elbowed him soundly in the side. But as the men loaded the sweet treat into their mouths, the friendly dispute ended as looks of pleasure came over both of their faces. Donato's eyes drifted shut as if he could savor the flavors better that way.

Warmth crept into Alejandra's chest. How different was her life now than just three months ago? Life had been steady enough with Papa in their little hut at Las Cuevas. But now, surrounded by this unlikely mixture of friends, a peace touched her spirit like she hadn't felt in a long time. If only Papa could be here to feel it, too.

A quiet sniff sounded beside her, and Alejandra glanced at Mama Sarita. The woman met her gaze, a lone tear trickling down her cheek. She reached for Mama's hand, and the older woman returned her squeeze. They'd lost so much, the two of them. But they had each other. And she wouldn't let that change.

Her eyes scanned the faces around the table again, snagging on the empty chair across from her. Edward. Anna had said he was called on an unexpected assignment this morning. What kind of work took a man from his family on Christmas day? Nothing respectable. That was for certain.

Señor O'Brien rose from his chair, and a hush came over the room. As he moved to a small side table in the corner, some of the men exchanged smiles. Did they know what was happening?

"Normally, Anna does the honors on Christmas," Señor O'Brien said as he picked up a stack of brown paper bundles and examined them. "But something tells me she's been on her feet more than she ought this morning, so I'm taking this job."

He began handing a package to each of the men. Not going down the row, but looking at the paper on each, then taking it to a specific vaquero.

Alejandra eyed Juan, who was one of the first to receive a paper bundle. His gnarled fingers fumbled with the paper, but he finally split the seam to reveal a bright red pañuelo. Or what did the Americans call it? A bandana. Something like that.

A smile split Juan's craggy brown face, lighting his eyes. He held the pañuelo up in one hand and a gold coin in the other. "Muchas gracious." He looked to Anna first, and then to Señor O'Brien who still passed out packages.

Anna's eyes shimmered as she met the older man's gaze. "You're welcome, Juan. It's only a small token, but given with all our love and appreciation."

Alejandra had to swallow down the lump in her throat. These people acted like part of the same family.

Someone tapped her shoulder. She turned to find Señor O'Brien holding a brown paper package out to her, a warm smile twinkling his blue eyes. "For you, Señorita."

What? She took the bundle without thinking. He moved on, leaving her to finger the coarse surface of the paper. The package was small—not much larger than the length and width of her hand. Alejandra glanced at Mama Sarita, who held a similar package, but she watched Alejandra.

"Open it, mija."

Her fingers found the slit, and eased the two edges apart. White cloth peeked up at her. Alejandra opened the paper wider...and gasped. A beautiful white handkerchief lay in her hands, edged in lace, and with her initials A.D. embroidered in lovely script in a corner. She lifted the fabric and fingered the delicate edging. Something hard rolled out, and Alejandra grabbed at it. She caught it by the edge, and raised up a shiny gold coin.

Turning to Anna, she found the woman watching her with a soft smile. "It's been a long-standing custom that Jacob's Pa would give the men a five dollar gold piece each Christmas. My first year here, when I was just the cook, I made them all a new handkerchief. Papa O'Brien's not with us anymore, but we love the traditions."

Alejandra gazed at the elaborate handkerchief in her hands, then looked back at Anna. "You made this? Anna, it's beautiful."

Anna's smile wobbled and her chin ducked just a bit. "You like it?"

"I love it." A rasp tinged Alejandra's voice, as the sting of tears burned her throat.

EDWARD nudged his horse into a canter as the Guadalupe River came into view on his right. After two weeks, he was getting close to home, and his muscles itched to be off the horse. If he was honest, they itched to take Alejandra in his arms, but that wasn't likely to happen. Not unless she'd had a sudden change of heart, or maybe hit her head with a frying pan. Not that he wished for the latter.

If she would just look at him without venom in her eyes. She acted like she had some kind of vendetta against him. Like she saw in him all the evil soldiers she'd met in the past. But how could a simple metal badge stir such a reaction? Whatever happened to her at the hands of soldiers in her past, must have been horrible, indeed.

As he neared the fencepost that marked the turn-off to the Double Rocking B, Edward reined his gelding down to a walk. The animal would need the long driveway to cool his muscles before they reached the barn.

The ranch buildings nestled at the end of the road struck a chord in his chest. He'd been gone a lot the last couple weeks since Christmas. Most of his trips lasted several days, and the most recent had kept him away almost a week. It had never bothered him before to travel all over the Southwest section of Texas. But the ranch had a new draw these days.

Alejandra was such an amazing woman. A hard worker, for sure. She had that house and kitchen in perfect order the first week she arrived. And her devotion and kindness to Mama Sarita were admirable. They weren't even blood relatives, from what he understood. She'd become a good friend for Anna too, especially now that the doctor told her to stay in bed until the baby was born. Not many women could be patient when Anna got cranky.

So why did she hate only him? He had to know. Had to find out how to fix this. Before it killed him.

After unsaddling the gelding and leaving him in Juan's capable hands, Edward jogged up the porch stairs and into the house. The place was quiet, almost eerily so. If Anna was following the doctor's orders, she would be in her bedroom on the lower level. He headed there.

Knocking on the open door, he peeked around the edge. "Anyone home?"

"Come in, little brother." Anna rested among the covers, her hair mussed and voice groggy from sleep.

"Did I wake you?" He stepped into the room and plopped on the chair near the bed.

"Not really. There's nothing to do all day except sleep and eat and sew." She pointed toward a mound of fabric on a trunk against the wall. "I've made enough baby clothes to last until the child turns twenty."

He offered a chuckle. "Where's your entertainment staff?"

"Mama Sarita and Alejandra took Emmaline to town with them. She's dying to see Aunt Laura, so I told them to spend the day."

Edward nodded. Now he could talk without being overheard. He leaned forward to rest his elbows on his knees. "Anna. Do you know what I've done to make Alejandra so angry?"

She raised both brows. Maybe his question had been a bit abrupt. No use beating around the bush, though. "What makes you think you've done something?" She tilted her chin suspiciously. "Is there something I should know about?"

He jerked back and held up his palms. "No, I haven't done a thing." He settled back with his elbows on his knees. "That I know of anyway. It's just...the first few times I saw her, she was plenty nice. Then that time she saw me riding out for work wearing my badge, she acted like I was gonna tie her up and haul her to jail. Ever since then, she gets spittin' mad just lookin' at me. Monty thinks she has something against soldiers, and my badge reminds her of it." He eyed her carefully. "Has she said anything to you about it?"

Anna sighed. The long, dramatic kind women do when they want you to know they're thinking hard about something. She gazed past him toward the open door, but her mind didn't seem to be where she was looking.

At long last, she focused on him. The sadness in her face caught his breath. "Edward. I wish I could make it better for you, I do. But it's not my story to tell. What I can say is, you need to find a way to prove to her you're a good soldier."

He met Anna's gaze, frustration welling in his chest. "But how do I do that? She won't get near me."

"I don't know, Eddie. I honestly don't. Have you prayed about it?"

He sat back in the chair. "Prayed? Yeah. I have. But God's not telling me what to do."

The corners of her mouth lifted a bit. "Keep praying. It has to come in His time. He'll make the way clear."

Anna's face pinched, and she slid a hand to the base of her huge middle.

Edward's heart seized. "What's wrong? Should I ride for the doctor?"

She grabbed his arm before he could jump up and head for the door. "No, silly. Just a twinge. This baby's as feisty as his daddy."

He scrutinized her, but she didn't look to be in pain anymore. If the baby was coming, the pain wouldn't go away so quickly, right?

"You must be hungry." Anna released his arm with a motherly pat. "I think there's some peach pie left from dinner last night. Why don't you bring us both a piece, then you can tell me about your latest Ranger adventure."

Peach pie. Yes, that was just the thing. He rose and strode toward the kitchen. But as he walked, Anna's words came back to haunt him. *Keep praying. He'll make the way clear.*

Pausing in the kitchen doorway, Edward surveyed the room that even smelled like Alejandra. *God. I don't know what to do. Please make the way clear. Show me how to help Alejandra.*

Chapter Twelve

A flash lit the night sky as a blast of gunpowder exploded near the shack in the valley below.

"Give it up, Matthews!" Edward called down to the source of the blast. "You're blocked in. Give yourself up." His breath clouded in the frigid mountain air.

"I ain't goin' nowhere with you, lawman." Another flash and boom from below.

"Dead or alive. It's your choice," he shouted back. He scanned the darkness below. No movement that he could see. Where was Lockton? The other Ranger should be in place by now.

A shouted curse echoed from the valley, followed by the sounds of a scuffle and winded grunts. That's what he'd been waiting for. Edward leaped forward, traipsed down the hill with his Winchester rifle at the ready. Matthews should be the only bandit in this grovel of a cabin, but a Ranger never took anything for granted.

By the time he reached them, Lockton had the thief on the ground with a knot of rope already started around the man's wrists.

"I'll take care o' this snake. You wanna check the cabin for the goods?" Lockton snarled as he yanked another loop tight. His scowl alone was enough to make some men turn themselves in.

Edward booted the cabin door open, and scanned the room with his rifle barrel. Nothing moved. He stepped in farther, and his ears picked up a noise. A soft whining drifted from the corner, behind the small round stove.

He advanced closer. A dog? There in a shredded flannel blanket, lay a fur-covered skeleton. The only sign it still lived was the slight *thump, thump* of its light brown tail as the animal looked at him with glassy, soulful eyes.

Edward dropped to one knee and reached to stroke the animal. It flinched from his hand, but didn't seem to have enough strength to move far. Poor thing. What had the man done to it? Its fur was cold, and patches were missing all over the dog's coat, but its tail still fanned across the blanket. The tail moved again, but it wasn't wagging this time. Was there something underneath?

In answer to his question, a tiny muzzle peeked out between the hair. The whine sounded again, and this time it was clear the noise came from the puppy that wriggled out from under the dog's tail.

Edward scooped it up as gently as he could, and cradled the cool body against his chest. It couldn't be more than three or four weeks old. The puppy was lean, but not nearly as emaciated as the mother. A surge of anger washed through him. How could any man, even a blackguard like Matthews, treat his animals with such complete lack of concern?

The mother dog lay still now, not even her tail moving. With one hand still cuddling the puppy, Edward stroked the coarse hair of the older dog. She responded with a slight dip of her nose. Her ribs were so pronounced, the skin pooled between each of them. Their outline barely rose and fell with each labored breath.

She wouldn't make it. The unfortunate animal was too weak. Even if he stayed an extra night to nurse her, she might not live until morning.

He placed the puppy next to its mother, then rose to his feet and turned toward the shelves that appeared to hold food stores. Maybe he could find something she could eat to dull the pain and hunger. After a quick search, the best option looked to be the pot of beans cooling on the back of the stove. He scooped some onto a tin plate, then lowered it to the dogs. The puppy had curled up in the crook of its mother's front legs, and watched him with wide eyes.

As Edward's gaze trailed up to the mother's pronounced ribs, his chest constricted. They didn't move. He held a finger under her nose, but no wind brushed his skin. The poor animal. She didn't deserve such a tragic ending.

After some prodding, he finally got the puppy to lick some of the broth from the beans. Lockton came in, and grumbled about having to search the cabin for stolen goods on his own while Edward played with the animals. But a look at the puppy seemed to soften even the seasoned lawman's tough heart.

Once they had the recovered loot loaded on their horses and Matthews tied on his own scrawny beast, they mounted and started up the winding trail. Lockton led Matthews' horse with Edward trailing them to keep an eye on the prisoner.

The puppy fit perfectly in the inside pocket of his coat and seemed to be content enough, except for an occasional whine. As soon as they got to the town on the other side of the hills, he'd buy some cow's milk to feed the tiny fellow.

But then what should he do with it? Find someone in town willing to take it in? And how good were the odds that it would end up like its mother, starving to death in a dirty shack? No, this puppy was going home with him. But what would he do with it when he left on assignments? Maybe Anna and Emmaline would have mercy on the little guy.

ALEJANDRA leaned to sweep under the smallest chair in the front parlor, while Emmaline chattered to her doll on the sofa across the room. The household had fallen into the habit of speaking Spanish most of the time since she and Mama Sarita came to live there. A practice that made things easier for Alejandra, but didn't much help her learn the American language. But Emmaline wasn't as fluent as the rest of them, and still spoke American when she wasn't talking directly to Alejandra.

While she worked, Alejandra strained to understand the child's words. Something about making tea and Papa coming home.

A dog barked in the yard, drawing Alejandra's attention to the window. The ranch had only one dog that she knew of, and he usually went out with the vaqueros to help with the cattle. Had Juan kept him in the barn today?

The animal barked again, an excited yip that seemed to be an alert. Alejandra strode to the window to get a better view of the yard. A rider dismounted, his broad shoulders recognizable even though his back was turned as he faced the dog. Edward. He held a hand to the animal, while his other gripped the side of his jacket. The dog raised up on his hind legs, peering inside Edward's coat. What in the world? Maybe he had a treat there for the animal. The way its tail wagged, that had to be the case.

Juan approached them and picked up the horse's reins, then stood to watch Edward and the dog. After a moment, he shook his head and walked away, a grin raising the corners of his mouth.

Edward straightened with a final ruffle to the dog's head. Holding his coat closed across his chest, he strode toward the house.

When his boot steps sounded on the front porch, Emmaline looked up from her doll. Seeing him through the window, she leaped from the couch and ran to the door. "Uncle Eddie!"

She threw herself at his legs, her little girl arms not reaching very far around. There was nothing quite like the love of a child.

Edward's gaze snagged on Alejandra's before he squatted down to Emmaline's level. "I brought a special present for you, Emmy-girl. But first, have you been good?"

Emmaline clasped her hands behind her back and nodded. "Uh-huh."

"And have you obeyed everything your mama and papa and Señorita Alejandra and Mama Sarita have said?"

Her head bobbed again. "Uh-huh. Now can I see the present?"

His mouth cocked, pressing a dimple in his cheek. "Okay, then." He opened his coat and reached into his pocket. Then pulled out...a dog. A little tiny puppy, just barely longer than his hand.

Alejandra gasped, but the sound was drowned by Emmaline's squeal. The girl reached to take hold of the animal, but Edward caught her hands.

"Whoa, slow down there. Just pet him like this." He cradled her tiny hand in his as they stroked the puppy.

Emmy giggled. "He's so soft."

The whole scene made Alejandra's lungs ache. How precious the little puppy was. Especially in the arms of the big, strong hombre, while cute little Emmaline stroked and talked to it. What was a soldier doing with a little puppy like that?

Soldiers killed, not rescued. But maybe as a gift for Emmaline, he was willing to make the effort to bring it home. Edward seemed to love his family, if no one else.

"You know what, Emmy-bug? This little guy's getting hungry. You wanna help me feed him?" Edward sat back on his heels, preparing to stand.

"What does he eat?"

He patted the lower pocket of his coat. "I have his favorite milk, right here."

Edward looked up at Alejandra then, and caught her watching them. She jerked her gaze away, but heat climbed up her back.

"Alejandra, would you like to come help us?" His voice deepened, becoming milky rich. Something in his tone reminded her of that day in San Antonio, when he helped her obtain the wagon to travel to Seguin. He'd been so helpful. So kind.

She kept her eyes fastened on the floor. "I, uh. I better not." Reaching for the broom again, she busied herself with the dust pile she'd created.

A long silence hovered, but she didn't look up.

Finally, Edward spoke again in a quiet tone. "Come on, Emmaline. Let's go get his food ready."

And then they were gone. Leaving Alejandra with only her memories to fill the void.

ALEJANDRA pushed the hair from her face with the back of her wrist, then thrust her hands into the soapy water again to finish scrubbing the pan from dinner. One stubborn strand of hair remained, tickling her nose. She blew, jutting her bottom lip so the air flew upward. That seemed to take care of the wayward tendril.

A giggle sounded in the hallway, followed by footsteps and voices as Emmaline promenaded into the room. As usual, she chattered like a magpie. But the voice that responded was not Mama Sarita's. Its tenor was deep and masculine, but not the child's father. What was Edward doing in her kitchen again?

Alejandra didn't turn around, but kept her ear tuned to what she could understand of their conversation. Emmaline prattled about the puppy and her doll and a lot of other words Alejandra couldn't understand.

But when Edward's next words came, they were in Spanish. "Alejandra, we just came in to feed the puppy. Is there anything we can help you with first?"

She whirled to face him. "Um. No." Why wouldn't her brain work? "No, I'm almost done."

"Okay, then. Just let us know if you find something."

He wanted to help? But that's what his brother paid *her* to do.

Alejandra turned back to the wash bucket, but her ears stayed tuned as Edward's boots clomped to the pantry, then back to the table. He and Emmaline settled down on the floor, and Alejandra snuck a peak to see them cross-legged.

Edward handed the puppy to Emmaline. "Here, cradle your arms like I showed you, and let the puppy rest on them. There. See how cozy he feels?"

He removed a lid from a jar, and poured milk onto a small plate. "Okay, now. Can you set him on the floor so we can help him eat?"

Emmaline gave the puppy a quick peck on top of its head, then placed him in front of the plate.

Edward guided the little guy toward the milk, and coaxed him to dip his snout in. The puppy must have dipped too far, because he came up sputtering and sneezing little white drops.

Alejandra bit her lip against a smile.

"Come on, fella. You'll like it once you try it," Edward crooned to the puppy. For such a big man, he was being incredibly gentle.

"He's doing it. He's drinking." Excitement laced Emmaline's words, as she rose to her knees and bounced.

"Easy there, cowgirl." Edward held up a hand to calm her. "We don't want to scare him."

The puppy seemed to have figured out how to drink the milk, because he lapped for several minutes while Edward held him in position. At last, the animal looked up from its dinner, then collapsed into Edward's hand.

"I think he might be finished." Edward scooped him up and snuggled him close, his gaze turning toward Alejandra.

Heat crawled up her neck. He'd caught her watching them. Again. She spun back to her work.

"Would you like to hold him, Alejandra?" The rich tone of Edward's voice stopped her movement. She forced herself to breathe.

"Come on, Miss Alejandra. He likes to lick my fingers." Emmaline giggled. "Maybe he'll lick yours, too."

Alejandra turned slowly back to them, the happy sounds pulling her like food to a starving child. Emmaline giggled again as Edward held the puppy up to sniff her ear.

One step at a time, her feet carried her toward them.

Emmaline patted the floor next to her. "Come sit next to me, and I'll show you how to hold it." She took the puppy from Edward as if she'd handled baby animals all her life.

"You have to make a cradle in your arms like this for him to snuggle into." The little girl demonstrated, a little rougher than the puppy might have liked, but it didn't complain.

"Like this?" Alejandra mimicked Emmaline's arms.

"Yes. Now you can hold him."

The puppy's warmth washed through Alejandra, and she snuggled it under her chin. The little fellow nuzzled her neck, then licked his rough tongue across her finger. She almost giggled the way Emmaline had. But on the heels of the laughter came a longing she hadn't felt in weeks. Rudy used to snuggle under her chin like this. Her precious cat. Was he safe now? Somewhere warm and dry, with a full belly and someone to

125

love him? She had to believe that. Anything else was too hard to imagine. Alejandra bit her lip to hold back the tears. She had to think about something else.

Emmaline reached to stroke the puppy, and Alejandra focused on the girl. A soft smile curved the child's mouth, and her blue eyes twinkled as she watched the animal.

Alejandra's gaze drifted to Edward—and collided with his warm brown eyes. Watching her. Something about the softness in his expression. The way his eyes glistened. The sting of tears burned again. He was being too nice. How could she hate the man when he was so kind?

But she had to stay strong. He was a soldier. And no matter what, she couldn't give him the satisfaction of seeing her weak.

Chapter Thirteen

TWO days later, Edward carried his bedroll in one hand and the puppy in the other, as he tromped down the stairs. "You hungry, fella? We'll stop outside for a minute, then see what we can round up for us to eat."

A blast of cold air slapped his face when he opened the front door. On the porch, Edward dropped his bedroll by the door, then jogged down the steps and set the puppy in a grassy area. "Do your business, boy. Tired of cleanin' up after you in my room." It was a good thing Anna wasn't up and around much, or she'd never stand for the dog in his bedchamber. But the puppy was just a little tike, not big enough to stay by himself in the barn.

He examined the sky. Low gray clouds seemed to press down on him. Looked like the first snow of the winter would come today. Not something he was looking forward to riding through. A gust of wind whipped him, and Edward wrapped his coat tighter around himself.

So that raised the question, what to do with the animal when he left today? He couldn't drag a dog around on all his assignments. Besides, after a few days of good food, the animal was almost too big to ride in Edward's coat pocket. So what now? Juan might not mind taking care of him. But the weather was too cold for a young puppy to sleep in the barn without the warmth of its mother. Maybe Anna would take pity on the poor thing. But her mind was pretty busy getting ready for the baby. Especially since Doc said the infant might come any day. And she wasn't supposed to be up and around, either.

So that left... Dare he even hope that Alejandra might be willing to care for the puppy? She'd seemed to enjoy holding it that one time she hadn't fled the room the moment he entered. Even got a little teary-eyed. Anna said the woman loved horses, and she seemed to have a soft spot for dogs, too. Maybe she'd do it for the puppy's sake, even if she wouldn't for Edward.

The puppy's deed accomplished, Edward scooped him up and headed toward the kitchen. Following the aroma of hotcakes to its source, he found Mama Sarita pouring batter in a frying pan, and Alejandra whipping something in a bowl.

"Mmm... Smells good in here."

Mama Sarita smiled over her shoulder. "Will you eat breakfast with the family? Or should we pack food for your trip?"

He exhaled. "Afraid I have to leave early again today."

She nodded. "We'll pack your satchel then."

Her hands flew as she flipped a batter cake in the frying pan, then smeared jam onto some that cooled on a plate, and rolled them into skinny tubes.

His stomach growled. Alejandra wrapped the stack of hotcake tubes in a cloth, then stuffed them in his burlap satchel, along with several other cloth-wrapped bundles. The women worked together without words, as though they could read each other's thoughts. Like magic. And he had a front row seat.

"Looks like it's going to snow today."

Mama Sarita looked up, the creases in her brow deepening. "You must be careful then. Can you stay home instead?"

Warmth stole over Edward's heart. "I'll be fine. Pepper and I have ridden through much worse."

When the bag was packed, Alejandra handed it to Mama Sarita, then stepped over to add more hot cake batter to the pan. Why wouldn't she give the satchel to him herself? Why did she avoid him like scarlet fever? It was frustrating, to be judged so harshly by a simple badge. Didn't she see he'd never hurt someone without just cause? Couldn't she tell he was different from the soldiers who had hurt her? He clamped his jaw.

Mama Sarita passed him the bag of food, and he realized he still held the puppy. Best to ask now and get it over with. Maybe Mama Sarita would be willing to care for the animal, even if Alejandra couldn't bring herself to.

"Do you think… I mean…would you mind caring for the puppy? While I'm gone? If it's not too much trouble." Heat flamed his neck. Why did he stammer like a school boy?

Alejandra's head came around, and a glimmer lit her eyes. But she didn't speak.

"Sì. Of course." Mama Sarita reached for the little guy where he snuggled against Edward's chest. The animal braced against her with his paws, but she scooped him up and cuddled him close. "Emmaline tells me she's been helping you feed him. It will be good for her to help us." Mama Sarita smiled at him, the lines around her eyes giving her the look of wisdom.

"Thank you." What else was there to say?

Mama Sarita still looked at him, but her smile had dimmed, a sadness shadowing it. Alejandra had turned back to her work, and wasn't looking at him at all.

He shuffled his feet. "Okay, then. I'll be off." Still nothing from Alejandra. But what did he expect? Hoisting the sack over his shoulder, he turned and trudged from the kitchen.

In the barn, he went through the motions to saddle Pepper. But his mind couldn't get past the image of Alejandra's back to him, and the sad smile that haunted Mama Sarita's eyes as she held the puppy. Was being a Ranger worth it? He thought back to his reasons for joining the force. Independence. And respect. Mostly respect, if he was honest.

He huffed a humorless chuckle. Alejandra didn't respect him, and his status as a Texas Ranger was the very reason. Life sure could be ironic.

But if he weren't a Ranger, what would he be? A cow hand on Jacob and Anna's ranch again? Go back to being "Little Brother?" After all his hard work to break free, he couldn't turn back.

So now what?

LATER that morning, Alejandra stroked the puppy as it slept in her lap. Tía Laura had come for a visit, and they'd dragged chairs into Anna's room so she could remain in the bed while they talked. The conversation had run mostly in American, and Alejandra strained to follow as best she could.

"Tell me what…town?" Anna's face held a perkiness that hadn't been there these last few days.

"Well." Tía Laura's brow furrowed as she thought through her answer. "Work…courthouse is…fast. Uncle Walter's store…bigger…building. He's…thinking to…serve…bank."

"Oh my." Anna's brows rose, and she pressed a hand to her chest. "That *is* news."

Pain crept through Alejandra's head. How could she ever catch all the words and interpret them, while still hearing what was being spoken next? And the worst of it, she still didn't understand enough to know what was really being said. Something about Uncle Walter's store and a bank and a courthouse. For all she knew, the man might be planning to sell out to the bank. Although that didn't seem likely.

After a while, Tía Laura paused in her speech, as if she'd exhausted her news. Her eyes took on a soft smile as the lines around them crinkled. "Where's Edward?"

"He's…assignment," Anna answered.

Tía Laura turned to Alejandra and Mama Sarita then, her words slowing and more pronounced. "Edward is so good…a Ranger, he makes…proud. I'm so glad he…his calling."

Alejandra's temples pulsed, as she struggled to understand the words. Was Tía Laura saying she was proud of Edward for being a soldier? How was that possible?

A frown settled over Anna's features, and she released a long breath. "I wish…dangerous." She must have noticed the look on Alejandra's face, because she turned to her and spoke in Spanish. "I was telling Aunt Laura that I am proud of Edward, but I wish his job weren't so dangerous. I sometimes long for the days when he used to work as a vaquero on our ranch."

So he had been a vaquero at one time. No wonder Edward fit in so well with the others here. "Why—" Should she really ask the question? Yes, Anna had always been open to telling anything. She started again. "Why did he leave the ranch to become a soldado?"

A thoughtful line creased Anna's forehead. "I suppose there were a couple of reasons. He needed to live his own life, for one. We moved here when he was fifteen, and he started working with Monty and the vaqueros right away. I was cooking here in the ranch house, though, where I could keep an eye on him." Her lips pinched in a guilty smile. "I was a bit overprotective at times.

"So when the Rangers built up their group a couple years ago, Edward jumped at the chance." Her head tilted. "I think the other thing he loves is the chance to help people."

Alejandra couldn't stop her brows from shooting up. "Help people? As a soldado?" The puppy in her lap raised its head and growled a complaint.

The corners of Anna's eyes crinkled. "Sì. Edward is one of the kindest people I know. As a Ranger, he captures the people who do wrong, so the good people can be safe."

Safe? That didn't match her experience with soldados. Could Edward really be so different?

EDWARD shucked his muddy boots on the front porch and rolled up the legs of his brown wool trousers. The snow from three days ago had only brought a couple inches, and now this frigid rain washed the last of the white powder away, leaving a dreary, muddy mess. He shook off his coat too, and laid it next to the boots. No sense in bringing it inside where the wet wool would leave a mess in the hall. A mess Alejandra would likely have to clean.

Alejandra. A warm anticipation sped up the thumping in his chest. But first he had to clean himself and get rid of these damp clothes.

A half hour later, Edward jogged down the stairs, fresher than he'd been in days. He followed the sound of women's voices to Anna's room, and found her and Mama Sarita sewing tiny shirts. He ambled over to where Anna lay in the bed, and planted a kiss on her cheek. "How's my best girl today?"

She swatted his arm. "Emmaline would be heartbroken if she heard you say that."

He stuffed his hands in his trouser pockets. "Where is Emmy-bug?"

Anna sank back into the pillows. "I think Alejandra finally got her to sleep for a nap. I don't know what I would do if I didn't have these two here to help with things." She waved toward Mama Sarita.

He nodded to the older woman. "We're awfully thankful for you both."

The lines around her eyes crinkled. "I wouldn't want to be anywhere else. Are you hungry? I think Alejandra's in the kitchen feeding that puppy. I'm sure she'd be happy to rustle up some grub for you, too."

Was that a twinkle in her eye? No matter, the invitation was just what he'd been hoping for. "Yes, ma'am." He tipped an imaginary hat, then headed out the open door.

The murmur of a soft female voice drifted from the kitchen, but quieted at the sound of his footsteps. His heart pinched. Why did Alejandra always seem disturbed by his presence?

He paused at the doorway to take in the scene. Alejandra sat in the middle of the floor, the puppy perched in front of her. She eyed Edward like a wild stallion locked in a corral—wary, and not willing to show fear or weakness.

"Hola." He spoke the simple greeting to her, then turned his attention to the puppy. This approach worked with wild horses. Maybe it would have the same effect on people. He dropped to his knees and held out a hand. "Hey there, fella."

The puppy kept its seat, but cocked its head as Edward cooed. Edward crept closer, keeping his hand outstretched. When he was within reach, the puppy pawed at him. Edward responded by scratching the soft golden fur behind his ears—a favorite spot for all dogs. "You like that, sì?" The little guy responded with a wide yawn.

"Is he crawling yet?" He flicked a glance at Alejandra, then focused on the animal again.

"Sì. He follows me around the kitchen while I cook. Always underfoot."

Despite her words, her voice held a loving tone. And who couldn't love something as cute as this little guy? At least she was talking, and hadn't jumped up and run yet.

"I was thinking, we need to give him a name. Any ideas? I'm not too good with this kind of thing."

She was quiet, and Edward fought hard not to look at her. The puppy nibbled on his fingers with wet gums. An adorable distraction.

"I don't know your American names, but I would call him Sol, because he's yellow like the sunshine." Her voice was strong, sure. And had the most beautiful cadence to it. He could listen to her all day if she would let him.

A grin tugged at the corners of his mouth. "Sol. I like it." He scratched under the puppy's chin. "What do you think, Sol? Perfect?" The animal let out a high pitched bark.

He glanced up to grin at Alejandra, and found a smile playing with the corners of her beautiful mouth. "He likes it."

"Sì."

Chapter Fourteen

A woman's cry pierced the kitchen walls—half scream, half moan. Alejandra wrapped her arms around Emmaline as the girl scrambled onto her lap. "It's all right, niña. Your mama's doing a great job, and I'm sure she'll be fine. It will be over soon, and you'll have a new baby to help take care of."

Oh, how she hoped her words would be true. Anna had to be fine. Women had babies all the time, and many of them came through with no problems. But not all. An invisible weight pressed down on Alejandra's shoulders. For once, she wished she could pray to a God who would take care of things. A God who would make things better.

It was awful to be so useless. She could do nothing to make sure Anna came through this healthy. But Doctor Steiner was with her. And Mama Sarita and Tia Laura. She couldn't ask for any better nurses for her friend. And it was Alejandra's job to keep Emmaline busy.

Another cry rent the air. This one snapping Alejandra from her thoughts. "Come on, Emmy. Let's go see how the horses are doing." She rose to her feet and clasped the girl's hand.

They went out the back door, the quicker to get outside and away from the heart-wrenching screams. Alejandra tried to keep up a steady stream of questions and conversation, but for once, Emmaline didn't seem inclined to talk. She didn't blame her. It was hard for Alejandra to pull her mind from what was happening in that bedroom. How much harder for this little girl who was so worried about her mama?

When they rounded the house, a figure paced the front porch. Señor O'Brien—or Jacob, as he insisted she call him. He paused when he saw them, and Emmaline raced up the stairs to throw herself in his arms.

"Papa!"

He scooped her up, and held her tight for so long, it was amazing Emmy didn't squirm out of his grip. But they both seemed paralyzed with fear. Alejandra had to do something to help.

"Emmaline and I were just going to the barn to pet the horses. Would you like to come with us?"

He hesitated, then looked back at the house. "No. No, I should stay here. Just in case."

Alejandra forced a smile onto her face. "Of course. You'll want to be ready the minute the doctor tells you whether it's a boy or girl."

"Sì." Jacob still had that hesitant, uncertain look on his face. He finally set Emmy down, then pointed her toward Alejandra. "Give the horses an extra pat for me?"

"All right." Emmaline plodded down the stairs obediently, and Alejandra took her hand again.

When they stepped into the barn, it took a moment for Alejandra's eyes to adjust to the dim light. As they did, the form of a man took shape, walking down the center aisle. Those shoulders. Her heart squeezed at the sight.

"My two favorite girls." The rich voice flowed over her, bringing heat to her face as the words sunk in. Surely he didn't mean her. He was just being kind. But a soldier? Kind?

"Uncle Eddie." Emmaline's voice lacked its usual zest, but she still flew to Edward, wrapping herself around his legs.

"Emmy-bug." He bent down so she could see the puppy in his arms. "Sol here was just asking for you."

Emmaline ruffled the animal's fur, bringing her face close to his and cooing. He responded by licking her nose. Instead of giggling like normal, she looked back at Edward, her voice taking on an unusual seriousness. "Mama's having the baby now. But I think it's bad, because she was screaming awful loud."

Edward's brow wrinkled as he studied the girl. Then he lowered himself to the ground and sat cross-legged, right there in the middle of the barn aisle. Wrapping a hand around Emmaline's waist, he settled her on his leg where she could still see him. "Emmy-girl, do you know it was just the same when you were born?"

Alejandra swallowed down a lump in her throat as the little girl shook her head, wide eyes focused on him. She couldn't help but stand mesmerized, watching Edward's tenderness with his sobrina.

"It was. And I was so scared something was wrong. Your mama's always been strong and brave. When I heard her cry like that, I just knew it was bad. But then I prayed, and asked God to keep her safe, and make you healthy. And the next thing I heard was a little tiny baby crying." He tickled her tummy, and Emmaline doubled over in a giggle.

When she recovered, she studied Edward's face again. "So God made her okay?"

Edward nodded. "Yes. And I think we should pray again. What do you say?"

Emmaline raised her face to Alejandra and reached out. "Miss Alejandra, come pray for Mama with us."

How could she deny such a request? She crept over and sat down on the ground. This dress was due for a washing anyway. She left as much space as she could between Edward and herself, despite Emmaline clutching her hand.

"Father, please be with Anna and the baby." Edward's strong voice washed through Alejandra. "Keep them healthy and make the hard work go quickly. In the name of Your son, Jesus. Amen."

"Amen." Emmaline released her hand.

Alejandra looked up, her focus pulled as if by a rope to the warm chocolate eyes of Edward Stewart. She might have fallen into that gaze, as deep as it was. The dark shadows under his eyes gave him a haunted look. What was it that plagued him? His sister? Out of the corner of her eyes, she saw the motion of his hand stroking the top of Emmaline's head. He did love his family. That couldn't be denied.

"Uncle Eddie, now that you prayed and Mama's going to be better, can we go see her?" Emmaline turned those blue eyes on her uncle again.

A smile tipped the corner of his mouth as he looked down at the child. "Soon, Emmy-girl. As soon as they call us. Shall we take Sol to see the horses first?"

"Yes." Emmaline scampered up, and Alejandra stood, too.

As she rose, a hand touched her elbow, assisting her efforts. She scrambled up, then spun to face Edward, breaking the contact. But those eyes caught her again, stopping her mouth before she could snap at him. The haunted expression. It pierced to the core of her being. Would his prayer make a difference? Would God listen to Edward better than he'd heard Alejandra all those years ago when Mama was killed?

A voice called from somewhere outside the barn, and Edward's head whipped to the side. Listening.

Alejandra held her breath to hear better. Yes, it was Mama Sarita. Calling Edward.

He shoved the puppy in her arms and took off in a sprint.

Alejandra reached for Emmaline's hand. "Come, niña."

When they made it to the front porch, Mama Sarita stood waving them in, a huge smile lighting her face. "It's a boy. And your mama's dying to see you, little one." Mama Sarita took the puppy from Alejandra. "She's asked for you, too, mija. Go see the babe."

Anna wanted to see her? Surely not. But Mama Sarita's eyes twinkled as she nodded toward the front door.

"Go."

Tiptoeing toward Anna's bed chamber, Alejandra met the doctor coming out.

"Go on in, but just for a moment." He motioned into the room. "Anna needs her rest, but she insists on seeing everyone first."

Alejandra stopped at the open door to examine the scene inside. Anna lay in the bed, eyes drooping and mussed brown hair no longer confined to a braid. In the crook of her arm lay Emmaline, her face upturned as she chattered to her mother in American. Jacob stood beside them, a sentinel on guard duty. One protective hand rested on his wife's shoulder, but his face shone with such pride it was impossible to miss.

Edward perched on the edge of the bed beside his sister, his back to the door. What relief must he feel, seeing her well and safe?

Alejandra searched the room for the infant. Anna's arms were empty. Panic welled in her gut. Where was the babe? Had something happened to it? But then she saw a corner of the blanket Anna had painstakingly crocheted, sticking out past Edward's arm. She crept inside, staying toward the outer edge of the room, moving around so she could get a better look at the bundle he held.

Anna motioned her over. "Come see, Alejandra. He's finally here."

She hated to come closer. This was their family moment. She couldn't intrude. But then the blanket in Edward's arms moved, and a little fist raised up from it. Curiosity pushed her forward, close enough she could finally see inside the bundle.

"Oh," she breathed. He was perfect. Such delicate, tiny features. His little nose, mouth, chin... All too precious for words. He opened his eyes, a dark smoky blue, and looked at her. Not an intense focus, but a vague, fuzzy gaze. A noise came from his mouth, an incoherent babble. But the look and the sound seemed to be a greeting.

"Hola, niño." She smiled at the babe.

He thrust his tiny hand in her direction, and Alejandra couldn't resist caressing it. His skin was softer than anything she'd touched.

"I think he likes you." Edward's voice was husky.

Alejandra glanced up to see him watching her, his brown eyes glistening with extra moisture. Heat slid up her neck. She should look away, but his gaze held her.

A dimple appeared in one of his cheeks as his mouth tipped. "God answered our prayer."

THE rest of the day, Alejandra watched for an opportunity to hold the babe for longer than a quick moment. But the first opportunity came that evening. Poor Anna was exhausted. The wee one seemed to be eating well and healthy, but hadn't settled down to sleep longer than a few minutes at a time. When Alejandra offered to care for the niño while his mother rested, Anna almost drifted to sleep before she could say yes.

Now, as she sat in the rocking chair in the main room, little Martin slept in her arms. She looked down into his perfectly formed face, and that ache formed again in her chest. The same knot that had started when she'd first touched his little fist. When the babe lay in the arms of his uncle Edward.

Had Edward's prayer made the difference in Anna's delivery? Or had she and the baby already been healthy, without the need of a God to intervene? As she watched the infant's delicate nose breathe in air, and his little mouth exhale, his tiny eyelids fluttered as a dream occupied his sleep. It was hard to imagine such a perfect babe could form without the help of a greater Power. Did God really know and care about little Martin? It seemed cruel, and a little impossible, to think He didn't. But what did that mean about her? Did God pick and choose the people He provided for?

Before she could examine the question any closer, light boot thumps sounded in the hall. Edward peered around the open doorway, a soft smile spreading over his face when he saw them. He sidled into the room, hands in his pockets as he ambled their way.

"There you are," he whispered when he was close enough to be heard. "I was looking for this little guy. Jacob wouldn't give him up earlier, so I thought I might get some nephew time now." He sank into the wingback chair beside Alejandra.

He wanted to hold the baby? But little Martin had just fallen asleep. And having the tiny bundle snuggled in her arms sent a warmth through her that she was loathe to give up. But she was only the cook and housekeeper. She had to remember that.

"Do...you want to hold him?" She couldn't bring herself to look at the man.

"No." A hint of a chuckle laced his voice. "I wouldn't dare disturb either of you."

Her gaze shot to his face. He was looking at the babe with such love shining in his eyes, it squeezed the breath from her chest.

Edward extended a hand to brush the feather soft hair that stuck out from the blanket wrapped around Martin's head. "I always wanted a little brother when I was younger." His voice was soft, throaty. "Someone to help bear the brunt of Anna's mothering. Mama died when I was seven, so that's when Anna grew over protective. And bossy."

Alejandra couldn't help another sideways glance at him. A smile curved his lips as he stared at the baby, but his focus seemed inward, somewhere far away.

"Looking back, though. Anna had a tough lot, becoming the woman of the house when she was only twelve. She did an amazing job at it. Even if she was a bit pushy sometimes."

A need burgeoned inside Alejandra. To defend Anna. To make sure he knew just how hard it was to grow up without a madre to love, to learn from, to be loved. And on top of the loss, she'd been expected to take over the running of a house. The cleaning and cooking. To fill such an immense void. She inhaled a strengthening breath.

"Your sister took on a woman's work at only twelve years old. I did the same, when my mama died. It is not easy, to be stripped of your childhood and your dearest friend, and be forced into the role of a grown woman, without anyone to show you the way. Your sister is strong and did what she had to do."

He was silent for a long moment. Had she offended him? But she didn't regret her words. He should know how amazing Anna really was. How hard her life must have been.

"I do know that now." His voice was barely more than a whisper. "I think I knew it even then. After Papa died in the war and our house was burned to the ground, all we had was each other."

His words pierced her chest, as if they'd been a bullet from a rifle. His father was killed, too? At the hands of soldados? But... How could he bring himself to wear the same badge? How could he become one of those that killed his own papa? None of it made sense. She opened her mouth to ask, but his words cut her off.

"I didn't realize you were the same age as Anna when you lost your madre. How did she die? From sickness?"

Her pulse thumped harder in her chest, as that old familiar heat washed through her. Alejandra's fingers crept up to the scar that marred her face. "No." The word croaked out. "The soldiers slayed her."

A sharp intake of breath sounded from the chair beside her. Alejandra dropped her hand and her gaze down to the babe. She'd said too much. What possessed her to share those details? Was he angry? She didn't dare look at him.

She had to get away before she said or did something she would forever regret. Lifting the warm bundle in her arms, Alejandra stood and placed little Martin in his uncle's arms. The babe shifted and made a noise, but his eyes never opened. She didn't dare look at Edward's face. She had to leave.

"I need to check things in the kitchen." It was as good an excuse as any. Alejandra spun and, without a backward glance, fled the room.

EDWARD stared at the empty doorway through which Alejandra had disappeared. When would she stop running from him? But at least she had shared some of her past this time. And the story was all too clear now. She'd touched her scar when she said the soldiers killed her mother. It must have been a horrible event. Did that explain the haunting in her eyes?

Especially when she looked at him. Does she fear him like she must have feared the soldiers all those years ago?

He dropped his head so it almost touched the baby bundled in his lap. *Oh, God. This is something only You can do. Soften her heart, Lord. Help her to forgive. Both the soldiers and…and You, Lord. Show me what I can do to help her trust again.*

Chapter Fifteen

THE next few days were a blur. Full of cooking and laundry, and cleaning when Alejandra could fit it in. Not to mention caring for that little rascal of a puppy while Edward was gone on another assignment. Emmaline became her constant companion, her own special helper and shadow, while the girl's mother adjusted to the new baby.

Martin was a fussy niño, louder than Alejandra had expected. Mama Sarita said it was colic, and she'd appointed herself as his nurse to relieve Anna of the full weight of his frequent tearful episodes.

With her efforts to keep the house running smoothly, Alejandra didn't get much chance to visit with her friend or the new babe. Sometimes Anna would bring him to the kitchen while Alejandra prepared the evening meal, but their conversations were never long, and Alejandra rarely had a chance to snuggle little Martin during one of his happier moments.

149

So when she crept into Anna's chamber to replenish the stack of clean diapers and found Anna awake, playing with the babe, Alejandra couldn't resist staying for a moment.

"Have you seen how big he's getting, Alejandra?"

"Sì. His little hands are growing chubby."

Alejandra watched over Anna's shoulder as her friend stroked a finger down Martin's cheek. He leaned into her touch, a hint of a smile flitting across his face.

"I think it tickles him," Anna said. She looked up at Alejandra. "Sit, please. Would you like to hold him?"

Alejandra sank onto the edge of the bed. Anna wrapped the blanket tighter around her babe, then placed him in Alejandra's arms. The little bundle was heavier than she expected, and she cradled him tighter. Martin snuggled into her side, sending a warmth flooding straight to her heart.

"There's nothing quite like holding a baby, is there?"

Alejandra looked up to see a sheen of moisture clouding Anna's eyes. The light there reflected the glow in her own chest.

"When I think back to my early days on this ranch..." Anna's voice softened. "Those first few times I ran into Jacob down by the Guadalupe River, I never would have dreamed we'd be married now with two beautiful little ones. It's like a dream come true."

Anna fell silent, then sniffed. "Have you been to see the river yet?"

Alejandra glanced up at the change in topic. "Not yet. There's been so much to do."

"What?" Anna's brow wrinkled. "Oh, no. We need to fix that."

A tap on the door interrupted Anna's next statement. She glanced at Alejandra with a raised brow.

Alejandra shrugged. Mama Sarita had taken Emmaline and the puppy for a walk since the sun was out today. Jacob was out with the rest of the vaqueros, but maybe he'd come back for something.

"Come in," Anna called.

Alejandra twisted to see the door as it creaked open. A rugged male face appeared in the opening. Edward. Several days' worth of beard shadowed his jaw, and tired lines etched the corners of his eyes. But her pulse picked up, just the same.

"Edward. When did you get back? Come see how much your nephew has grown." Anna waved her brother into the room.

"Just unsaddled Pepper, so I'm trail dirty. Had to stop in and say hola, though." His eyes met Alejandra's and locked there, as he strode around to stand beside his sister. A twinkle glistened in their depths, as if in a silent greeting intended only for her.

She fought to pull her gaze away, but couldn't. Why did her insides flip when he looked at her?

Edward finally dropped his focus to the babe in her arms, and Alejandra inhaled a long, quivering breath. "Hi there, niño." His tone raised a notch as he bent to speak to Martin.

With his head down, Alejandra's gaze fell on Edward's thick brown hair, mussed into loose curls from the wind and who knew what else. Her fingers itched to run through their masses. She tightened her grip on the blanket.

Stepping back, Edward turned to study his sister. "How are you, hermana? Feeling better?"

Anna's mouth formed the shape of a smile, but the dark skin and lines under her eyes told a different story. "Sì. I'm well. Just tired."

Edward nodded. "I'll leave you to rest then." He turned and started for the door.

"Eddie, before you came in, Alejandra mentioned she still hasn't seen the Guadalupe yet. Would you mind taking her?"

The man's eyes found Alejandra's.

She jerked her gaze away before she became trapped again in those chocolate depths. "It's okay, Anna. I'll wait until you're well enough to go with me. You'll want to see it, too."

Anna tossed her words aside with a wave. "That will be weeks—maybe months. Edward, there might be cinnamon pie left in the kitchen, then you could take Alejandra to the river. I told her to ride the Palomino mare any time she wants, but I don't think she's stopped working long enough."

"No." Bile churned in Alejandra's stomach at the thought of being alone with the soldier. "I can't go now. I need to help with the baby. And Emmaline will be back any minute. I need to press the laundry, and make tortillas for dinner."

Anna leaned forward and took the babe from Alejandra's grasp. "Mi hijo is ready to eat now, then he and I will both take a nap. Mama Sarita told me earlier that she was going to let

Emmaline make shapes in the tortilla dough." She leveled a stern gaze on Alejandra. "And you are going to the river if I have to make the men tie you to a horse."

Alejandra nibbled her lip to keep it from smiling at her friend's forcefulness. One of the things she'd missed the most lately was staring across the Rio Bravo at the giant Las Cuevas ebony tree that stood guard over the flowing water. Even now her chest tightened at the memories. She glanced up at Anna, who watched her, brows raised.

"Sí. I will go." Was she making the right decision? He must be safe if Anna trusted him. Right?

Her friend's face softened into a wide grin. "Good. Would you mind cutting Edward a piece of pie while he cleans up a bit? And ask Juan to saddle the Palomino for you."

Alejandra rose from the bed and turned to find Edward watching her. His mouth curved softly, but his eyes held a mixture of emotions she couldn't quite discern.

UNDER the brim of his hat, Edward glanced at the woman riding beside him. At last, a chance to spend time with her. God must be softening her heart—and answering his prayers. He couldn't have picked a better spot than the Guadalupe River, either. It was the prettiest place around, even in the middle of winter. He fought to keep the swell in his chest from spilling onto his face. That's where Jacob had courted Anna all those years ago, and it worked out well for them.

A squirrel scampered across the trail in front of them, and Edward's mare flinched. The animal's muscles tightened underneath him, sending tension through the reins in his hand. He sat deep in the saddle, anchoring his weight in his heels. Animals could smell nerves, so the more a rider relaxed, the better. He shot a look at the Palomino Alejandra rode, but that mare plodded calmly with nothing more than a flick of her ear. The old girl had been down this trail more than once in her dozen years.

His gaze drifted to Alejandra. She was so beautiful, with her delicate profile framed against the light gray of the sky behind her. Wisps of long black hair had escaped her coil, floating down her back. She sat straight and comfortable on the horse, her body settling into the rhythm as if she were part of the animal. She'd been a little unsure about the saddle when she first mounted. Were the saddles different in Mexico? His focus wandered back to her face. She'd not spoken except a few terse answers as he held the horse for her at the ranch. Maybe she'd loosened up some by now.

"Did you ride often at the ranch where you lived in Tamaulipas?"

The stiffening of her back was so slight he almost missed it. "Sì. We were allowed to ride Las Cuevas horses any time."

"That's good. And they provided saddles and bridles for you to use?"

A small shake of her head. "No. The vaqueros owned their own equipment. I rode with a halter made of rope."

He arched a brow. "You didn't use a saddle?" That would explain her excellent posture.

"No. Papa needed our saddle for his work. I only rode in the mornings after my duties were finished. And I preferred to ride without the thick leather separating me from the horse, so I can better feel the animal as it speaks to me." A hint of pink brushed her cheeks, and her chin dipped slightly. Was she embarrassed about what she'd said? Or just that she'd spoken more than a single sentence without being forced? At least he'd found a topic she cared about.

"How large was Rancho Las Cuevas? Were there many horses there?"

"Sì. There were many thousand cattle and..." She paused, twin lines forming between her brows. "...maybe five hundred horses in all. But not so many at the outpost where we lived."

"Did you have a favorite horse?"

The corners of her beautiful mouth lifted slightly. "I did not get to ride the same horse always. Only what was not being used by the vaqueros. There were a few I enjoyed very much."

Watching her face as she spoke was like observing an elegant minuet. Her eyes sparkled and her features danced across her face in perfect synchronization. If only he were standing in front of her, not riding beside, craning his neck to take in every breathtaking feature. Still, he'd relish every minute with Alejandra.

What else could he ask about the ranch that would keep her talking? Or maybe something about her stay at the Double Rocking B? He could ask about how she was faring with Emmaline, but it was obvious the girl adored Alejandra, and the feeling seemed to be mutual. The puppy. He hadn't even seen the little guy since he'd come back from his last assignment.

"So how's little Sol doing these days? Is he behaving himself with the new baby in the house?"

"Sí." The smile touched her face again, a little brighter this time. When she turned and glanced at Edward from the corner of her eye, his stomach did a little flip. "He is muy bueno. Always underfoot and chewing on things he shouldn't. He steals Emmaline's doll every chance he has, and took one of Mama Sarita's shoes while she napped yesterday. But he's too cute to be angry with."

Edward chuckled. "I suppose I should make him something to chew on. Is he getting bigger?"

Alejandra's eyes widened. "So big you won't believe it. Soon, he'll grow into those enormous paws."

They were close enough to the river now to hear the rustle of water, although a few trees still blocked their view. When the trail opened into the wide clearing that lined the riverside, a gasp sounded from beside him.

"Es hermoso." Their horses were just close enough for him to hear the breathy words.

Edward nodded. Yes, the sight was beautiful. The dark blue of the water stretched about thirty feet wide here, with trees and a few large rocks lining the other side. A bright red bird twittered on the branch of a live oak near them. The tree was massive, it's exposed roots supporting part of the river's bank, as if the river had grown up around the tree. An aura of peace permeated the entire scene.

Alejandra leaned forward to dismount, and Edward hastened to do the same so he could assist her. By the time he slid off and strode around the front of his mount, Alejandra was already on the ground and gathering her horse's reins.

"I'll tie the horses." He reached for the ribbons she held.

She glanced at him, eyes widening as if she just remembered he was there. "Sì. Gracias." After handing the leathers to him, she stepped forward to the river's edge while he led the animals to the live oak. When they were secure, he ambled over to Alejandra, careful not to disturb her revelry.

They stood for several moments, side by side, looking out upon the water. What he wouldn't give to know her thoughts. But he could be patient. She deserved that.

At last she repeated her earlier words. "It's lovely." When she turned her gaze to him, Edward sank into their liquid depths, the color of a dark coffee.

"It's so much like the Rio Bravo. Many times I would ride to the river's edge, and sit for hours. There was a huge old tree on the far side." She motioned toward the live oak where he'd tied the horses. "Much like this one. I used to imagine all the scenes that tree had seen. Children swimming in the river. Men watering cattle. Wild deer coming to drink. Sweethearts picnicking."

Her cheeks tinted pink at the last reference, and she grew quiet for a while. Then her mouth tilted on one side as she surveyed the tree. "The funny thing. Always before, the tree was far away. On the Texas side." She swept her hand toward the tree again. "Now I am here with it."

Turning back to the river, her eyes looked out across the expanse, and her voice took on a dreamy quality. "It is a beautiful land, our new home."

The words washed through Edward like a warm soup on a cold day. Soothing. Filling his heart with hope. She was beginning to think of this place as home.

A smile crept across his face. "Sí. It's beautiful."

Chapter Sixteen

TWO weeks later, Alejandra kneeled before the fireplace in the main room, scooping the small shovel deep into the cold ashes. She eased the full shovel out, and tilted it over the bucket, clamping the brown paper over the opening as the fine ash rose in a cloud. Wrinkling her nose, she fought the tickle of powder that escaped. She held the paper still until the cloud inside had time to settle, then extracted the shovel, and replaced the paper over the bucket. No sense in making more of a mess than she had to.

A hoarse, barking cough sounded from the next room over. Anna's chamber. The tiny sound had to be baby Martin, and it had been frequent for the quarter hour she'd been working in this room. Had he succumbed to the same illness Anna had been fighting the last few days? She'd said it was only a cold, but the cough that drifted from that room sounded like more than a cold.

Alejandra set the shovel aside and wiped her hands on her apron as she rose to her feet. Maybe there was something she could do to help with the baby. Did Mama Sarita know of a *medicina* she could make to ease the coughing?

She tapped on the door, but the coughing sounded again, drowning out her knocks. Pushing it open, she stood in the doorway to take in the scene. Mama Sarita paced at one end of the room, Martin propped on her shoulder as she bounced and soothed. A sniffle sounded from the bed, where Anna lay against pillows with a cloth to her nose. Were her nose and eyes red from tears or the sickness?

That high-pitched hoarse barking sounded again, and Alejandra's gaze shot back to the babe. His whole body wracked with the noise, and after three coughs, he sucked in deep gasps of air.

In four long steps she was by his side, propelled by the knot in her stomach. She couldn't stand there and do nothing while little Martin could barely breathe. "What can I do to help?"

Mama Sarita turned, still swaying and bouncing as she soothed the baby with a hand on his back. "We should go prepare medicine." The look in Mama Sarita's eyes, along with the deep lines taking hold on her forehead, tightened the knot in Alejandra's midsection. When Mama Sarita was worried, things were bad.

"Tell me what to make."

But instead of answering, Mama Sarita turned to Anna, whose pale skin almost blended with the white blanket

160

wrapped around her. "I'll take Martin with me to the kitchen as I tell Alejandra how to make the remedy."

Anna only nodded as her teeth began to chatter. She was in a bad way, too.

Alejandra grabbed a blanket from the foot of the bed and spread it over the other quilts that covered her friend. "Can I do anything for you?"

"T-t-take care of m-my baby."

"Sí." Alejandra smoothed the hair from Anna's forehead, and almost jerked her hand back from the heat there. "I'll be back soon with broth for you."

Anna didn't respond, except for her shivering, as her eyelids drifted shut.

That pitiful barking cough sounded again from behind Alejandra, squeezing her heart. She turned from her friend and strode toward the door, motioning for Mama Sarita to follow.

Once they'd traversed the short hallway to the kitchen, Alejandra spun to face her friend. "What should I do?" Her eyes drifted to the babe. A wheezing noise accompanied his every breath. They had to help him.

"Get out the largest pot, and fill it with water. Stoke the stove fire with as much wood as will fit in the opening. We need the water to boil quickly."

Alejandra was in motion before Mama finished speaking. The fire in the large cook stove had died to mostly white coals, as she was letting it go out so she could clean the ashes. What awful timing. She balled the last of her brown paper and built a teepee of bark around it. As soon as the fire took hold, she added a small piece of dried split wood. Good. Now for the pot.

As soon as she had the cast iron crock full of water and settled on the front of the stove, Alejandra checked the fire and added several more pieces of wood.

"Alejandra."

She spun to face Mama Sarita, who had draped a quilt over little Martin. It rose and fell with each raspy breath that sounded from the fabric.

"Ride out and find Jacob. Tell him to send for the doctor. I'll do my best to ease the babe's breathing, but he needs medicine."

The knot in Alejandra's stomach grew even larger. A doctor? Just hearing the word took her back to when the doctor had tended her that awful day when she was twelve years old. Her hand stole up to her cheek.

"Go."

The single word kicked her into action. Alejandra strode down the hall, trying to keep her footsteps light so she didn't scare Anna. Grabbing her cloak from the peg by the front door, she slipped outside. A cold wind blasted her, but she pushed through it as she sprinted to the barn. Inside, Juan poked his head from one of the stalls.

"I need to borrow the Palomino," she panted. "The baby's sick, and I need to find Jacob to get the doctor."

His face clouded, but his pace quickened as he picked up a rope halter and slipped back into the stall he'd just left. A moment later, he strode out, pulling the golden-colored mare behind him.

"I just need a bridle. I'll ride bareback."

He shot her a raised brow look, but reached for a leather bridle and slid it onto the mare's head.

After boosting her onto the horse's back, Juan patted the animal and looked up at her. "Via con Dios."

"Sí." She squeezed her heels into the mare's sides, and they were off at a canter.

It wasn't until she'd been riding for several minutes, that Alejandra realized she should have asked Juan if he knew where the men were working today. She'd never been anywhere on the ranch except to the river that day with Edward. She'd head in that direction. But Anna said this ranch covered hundreds of acres, spreading in all directions.

She reined the horse to a walk and looked around. No cattle or horses were in sight. Had the men said which way they were going that day? In her mind, she replayed the scene at the table that morning.

Paco had taken an extra serving of hotcakes, saying he needed meat on his bones since the temperature had dropped. Monty elbowed the man and said he should be thankful he didn't have to chop ice in the river yet. Did that mean the cattle were being pastured beside the river?

That might be as good a place to start as any. Besides, that was the one trail she knew, and wouldn't have to worry about getting lost.

When she reached the start of the trees that lined the river, Alejandra reined the mare to a halt. The ground didn't show any fresh hoof prints, especially not what she'd expect from hundreds of cattle.

Alejandra scanned the landscape in the other directions. The pasture continued to her right, curving around the trees as it opened into a wide grassland. Maybe she should follow the tree line in that direction. The herd could be around the bend.

A single snowflake drifted down in front of Alejandra, shifting her focus to the sky above. Several more flakes floated from the low gray clouds. Perfect.

After following the trees for about five minutes, tiny specks appeared in the distance, loosening some of the tension that spread across Alejandra's shoulders. The cattle. She pushed the mare into a run.

Soon, one speck separated from the rest, cantering toward her. Jacob met her halfway, reining in his pinto. "What's wrong?"

"We need a doctor." She fought to control her panting. "The baby's cough is much worse, and he's not breathing well. Anna's in bed with a fever."

Jacob spun his horse and yelled to Monty, who had ridden up behind him. The men conversed in American for a quick moment, then the foreman wheeled his horse back toward the herd.

Jacob waved a hand as he kicked his horse. "Come on. Let's get to the house."

Alejandra pushed her horse, but the winded Palomino mare couldn't keep up with Jacob's muscled pinto. And he didn't slow down to wait for her. Not that she wanted him to. The panic that twisted his face when she'd delivered her message had intensified her own fear.

Juan was walking Jacob's gelding when she reined in at the ranch yard. He took her horse as well, and nodded toward the house. "You let me take care of these two. You're needed more inside I'm sure."

Once in the house, Alejandra followed the sound of voices to the kitchen, where Jacob stood with his son in his arms. He held the babe near the stove, in the path of steam wafting from the pot of water. Emmaline sat at the table, munching a slice of bread and watching the scene with wide eyes. If her disheveled hair told the story correctly, she must have just woken from her nap.

Mama Sarita ladled something into a cup, but looked up when Alejandra stepped in the room. "Mija, take this broth to Anna. You may need to feed her if the fever is too high."

OVER the next three hours, Alejandra helped where she could, flitting back and forth between Anna's chamber and the kitchen. Cool damp rags to cool Anna's burning face, as much drinking water as she would swallow, a fresh sleeping gown to replace the sweat-soaked one that clung to her.

The steam finally seemed to help baby Martin breathe easier. And the intense relief that flooded her chest was mirrored in the sagging lines of Mama Sarita's face.

"Gracias, Dio." The older woman breathed the prayer as she swayed back and forth with the child laying against her shoulder. He'd fallen into an exhausted sleep, his back rising and falling with each ragged breath.

Emmaline wasn't speaking much, but still sat at the table with blue eyes wide and the puppy in her lap, her doll clutched against her. As soon as Alejandra slid the pans of cornbread batter into the oven, she moved to the table and settled into the chair beside the girl. Alejandra stroked a strand of fine brown hair out of the child's face.

"Do you smell that stew simmering, Emmy? There's nothing that smells better than a beef stew." Alejandra smiled at the girl and reached for her hand. But Emmaline climbed onto her lap, snuggling in as Alejandra wrapped both arms around the child and the dog. The warmth that flowed through her was enough to offset the coldest blizzard.

Sol, disrupted from his sleep by the shuffle, opened his toothless puppy mouth in a wide yawn. Shaking his head, he looked around in that head-tilting way puppies do, then lay back down and chewed on Alejandra's hand. Resting her head against Emmaline's, she inhaled the little girl scent.

Emmaline was the first to break the silence. "Alejandra, can we pray for Mama and baby Martin?"

166

The child's quiet words stiffened Alejandra's shoulders. Could she pray? It had been so many years. And God hadn't listened to her prayers before. Maybe He would hear those of this child.

"Sí. I'll listen while you pray."

"Dear God." Emmaline's quiet voice was muffled as she lay against Alejandra's shoulder. "Please help Mama feel better, and baby Martin, too. Help him not to cough anymore, so we don't have to worry. Thank You. Amen."

LATER that evening, Alejandra sat on the edge of Anna's bed while the other woman ate beef stew. The doctor had come and gone, leaving a tincture of medicine for Anna, and instructions to place a drop in the child's mouth if his coughing continued. He'd said it was a good thing the baby had been born already bigger than most, or he may have been too weak to endure the sickness. Anna's fever seemed much better, but her eyes still held that glassy, red-rimmed look of sickness.

"Martin is still sleeping?" Anna seemed to search Alejandra's gaze for the truth.

"Sí. His papa is rocking him in the big room. His breathing is better, and I haven't heard him cough in a while."

The answer seemed to satisfy Anna, because she took another bite of the stew. "I'm sorry you have to nurse us both. But I must say I'm thankful you and Mama Sarita are here. I'm not sure what we would have done without you."

Alejandra ignored the compliment. "It's hard to watch the niño pequeño struggle so. I'm glad he's better."

Anna nodded. "Yes, it's awful being so helpless. I'm just thankful God had it under control."

Under control? "If God is taking care of things, why is the babe sick at all?" Alejandra couldn't keep a hint of bitterness from her voice.

Anna settled her spoon into the bowl in her lap, then sank back against the bed. Oh, no. Alejandra hadn't meant to upset her. When would she learn to keep her thoughts to herself?

"I guess I can't answer that." Anna didn't sound angry, but thoughtful. Her gaze searched out Alejandra's face. "I don't know why Martin is so sick at only three weeks old. But I do trust that God has the situation in hand. I've seen Him work amazing miracles, and His master plan is much better than anything I would have thought of."

Anna's voice grew softer. "Sometimes hard things happen to mold us. But if there's one thing I've learned through the years, no matter what happens, I'd rather be in God's hands than anywhere else." A smile touched her fever-chapped lips.

I'd rather be in God's hands than anywhere else. Alejandra stared at Anna as the words tumbled through her mind. Anna

168

had been through so much in her life. Family members died through terrible events, her family home burned. She'd been forced to move to a strange land, then endured any number of rough hardships on the ranch. All those things happened against her will. Outside of her control. So how could Anna say she'd rather be in God's hands than anywhere else? Hadn't God let these things happen?

"Look around you, Alejandra." Anna waved a feeble hand. "Look at all the ways God has blessed me. Jacob is the man of my dreams. This ranch. My precious children. None of these would have happened unless I'd gone through the bad, as well as the good." She slipped her hand into Alejandra's. "I can trust God. He loves me. And He loves you, too. Trust Him."

Trust. Could she do it?

Chapter Seventeen

TWO days later, Alejandra wiped the counter with a damp towel, then hung it from the oven handle to dry. The breakfast casseroles had been a hit with the men that morning. Especially with the avocado Edward brought back yesterday from his trip. Eating the creamy fruit was like a taste of home, recalling so many good memories and sensations. It had been one of Papa's favorites. And she would fry it with guavas and bananas for special breakfast tacos on his birthday.

A squeal broke her thoughts, and Emmaline's thundering steps pounded down the hall.

"Alejandra. We need cookies. Fast." She grabbed the doorway, panting.

A chuckle followed her down the hallway, accompanied by boot thumps. Edward's broad frame appeared in the doorway, setting off the flutter in her chest his appearance usually elicited. "We're riding out to see the cattle, and

Emmaline's afraid she might blow away if she doesn't have your cinnamon cookies to hold her down."

Emmaline giggled. "That's not true, Uncle Eddie." She turned her piercing blue eyes on Alejandra. "But can we take cookies, please?"

Alejandra was already lifting two cheesecloths from a shelf, as her mouth pulled into a smile. There wasn't a soul alive who could resist that little angel. After splitting the plate of cookies between the two cloths, she tied them, then turned with one in each hand. "All right. One to eat." She handed that one to Emmaline. "And one to share with your papa and the others."

Keeping that bundle in hand, Alejandra narrowed her eyes at Emmy. "Entiendes?"

"Sí. I understand." Emmaline's brown braids bobbed along with her chin. The child reached for the second bundle, but Alejandra jerked it from her reach and held it out to Edward. "We'll let your uncle carry them, just in case." She tweaked Emmy's nose.

The girl responded by wrinkling it, and Alejandra couldn't help but chuckle. She was so fun to tease.

"You might need to ride along with us to make sure she shares." Edward's deep voice brought Alejandra's head up.

"Yes, Alejandra. Please?" Emmaline grabbed Alejandra's arm and bounced up and down. "You've never been riding with us. You'll love it. I know you will. I'll show you Papa's cows, and he said there's a new baby one. You have to come. Please?"

Alejandra leaned away from Emmaline's exuberance, trying to gather her thoughts. Go on a ride with Edward and

171

Emmaline? It was a beautiful day out, especially for mid-February. And she hadn't been on a horse since that crazed ride to find Jacob and send for the doctor. But did she dare ride out with Edward again? They would have Emmaline with them this time. The child could be a sort of buffer. She chattered so much when she was excited, Alejandra would never have to speak a word. Just enjoy the ride.

She released a breath. "Sí. I will go."

Alejandra barely had time to prepare herself before Emmaline threw her little body into Alejandra's arms. "Oh, I'm so glad! It's going to be perfect. You'll see."

JUAN met them in the yard leading Pepper, Edward's horse.

"Would you mind saddling the Palomino mare for Alejandra to ride?" Edward asked as he took the reins from the older man.

"Un momento." Alejandra stepped forward. She avoided Edward's gaze as she spoke in a quiet voice to Juan. "I don't need a saddle. Just bridle, please, Señor."

He hesitated, so she sent him a pleading smile. Feet shuffling in the dirt, he cut a glance at Edward.

"You heard the lady." Edward clapped the man lightly on the back.

Juan's shoulders relaxed, and he bobbed his head. "Sí. I'll be right back."

While they waited, Emmaline stroked Pepper's face and kept up a steady monologue to the animal. "I'm going to ride on you with Uncle Edward. I can't ride you by myself yet, but you're my favoritest horse ever. We're going to see the cows, and share cookies with the cowboys. You're going to love it."

Juan appeared soon with the Palomino, and Alejandra took the reins. She motioned for him to help Edward and Emmaline first. It would be much easier to mount by herself, but it wasn't very lady-like. Best done while the others were distracted.

When Emmaline was settled on the gelding's back behind Edward, he secured her grip around his waist, then looked over at Alejandra. His eyes widened as he took in her position atop the mare. Then a corner of his mouth pulled, creating that dimple that always made her stomach flip. This time was no exception. She looked away so the butterflies would stop. Why did she let this man affect her so?

"Goodbye, Mister Juan." Emmaline waved and sent a beaming smile over her shoulder as they guided the horses from the ranch yard.

On the trail, they kept to a steady walk, covering terrain Alejandra had never seen. As expected, Emmaline carried the weight of the conversation, chattering about the puppy, her baby brother, the flowers she'd picked along this trail last year, and anything else that popped into her mind.

That left Alejandra to savor the fresh air, the warmth of the horse beneath her, and the freedom of the open land. Most of the area they traveled was gently sloping hills, with thick tufts of grass scattered across rocky soil. Occasionally, they passed patches of trees, with green pines interspersed amongst the dull brown of leafless branches.

Edward pointed to a section of forest. "There's a patch of Dogwoods in there. The prettiest pink and white flowers you've ever seen."

She eyed him. "Dogwoods?"

"It's a small, round tree. Doesn't have a purpose that I know of, except to look pretty. It does that job well, though." He sent her a cock-eyed grin, his dimple flashing again, and once again her stomach flipped.

Soon, they rode up on the herd. Jacob came to meet them, a wide smile spreading his face.

"Papa!" Emmaline bounced behind Edward.

He settled a hand on her leg. "Easy there, cowgirl. Don't scare Pepper."

"You came at just the right time, Emmy-girl." Jacob rode next to Edward's horse and scooped his daughter off the back, settling her in the saddle in front of him. "Another calf came last night, and it's ready to meet you."

Emmaline beamed. "Can I see it now? We brought you cookies, too. Alejandra came to make sure I share."

Jacob glanced up at Alejandra with a chuckle. "It's a good thing. Come on, little bit. Monty has something to show you first."

174

Alejandra watched the pair ride away. It was amazing how Jacob's face lit when he spoke to his daughter. She obviously held his heart.

A lump formed in her throat. Would she ever have a child of her own to love?

"Special, isn't it?" Edward's rich voice rumbled from behind her, washing through her like a warm blanket on a cool night.

The lump wouldn't let her speak, so she nodded. A stinging burned her eyes, but she blinked it back. No need to get sentimental about something she couldn't control right now. Squaring her shoulders, Alejandra scanned the vast herd in front of them. There had to be more than a thousand cattle in this pasture alone. Their long horns extended so far, they looked almost too heavy for the animals' gangly bodies. Although these cattle seemed a little more filled out than those at Rancho Las Cuevas.

"Shall we ride over and see the new calves?" Edward eased his horse up beside hers.

"Sí." Alejandra guided her horse into step behind his gelding as they worked their way around the edge of the herd.

"In the early days after I started riding with the cowpunchers, Jacob saved my hide from a wild cow right over there." He pointed toward a stand of forest a stone's throw from them. Underbrush grew thick between the tree trunks, giving it a dark, ominous appearance.

"A wild cow?" She turned a raised brow on him.

175

One side of his mouth pulled. "Well, she wasn't wild by nature. She was one of the ranch stock, but she'd caught her horns in some vines and been fighting against them for hours. When I rode up on her, she was mad enough to spit in the devil's face. She raised such a fuss, her horns finally came loose. She decided to take her displeasure out on me and my horse, but the fool mare wouldn't stay around for it. Left me in the dust, and that's where I'd still be if Jacob hadn't come along with some fancy roping."

A light danced in Edward's brown eyes as he finished the story. He was so handsome, especially when his smile reached his eyes. And those dimples. *Muy guapo.*

In moments like this, it was hard to remember why she didn't like him.

"THE filthy blackguard should be holed up just over this cliff."

Edward's muscles tightened at the growled words from the fellow Ranger riding behind him. This was it. They'd already nabbed the man's two accomplices who'd helped him pull off the five bank robberies. And now this was the end of the line for ol' Blackie.

Leaning forward in the saddle, Edward did his best to assist his horse as they climbed a steep, rocky embankment. Pepper was usually sure-footed, but this hill would be a challenge for any mount. Near the top, he eased back on the reins and slid off his gelding. "Stay here, boy." He kept his tone low as he tied the animal to a short pine tree.

Extracting his Winchester from the sheath on his saddle, Edward crept the remaining distance to the top of the ridge. Townsend stayed close behind him as they sidled to a boulder that would offer some cover. They had to get the drop on this guy.

Edward scanned the valley below. A small cabin nestled in a dusty yard where a few tiny dots wandered around. Probably chickens pecking at insects or other vermin. A horse and cow grazed a distance away from the building. There wasn't a fence to contain the animals. Were they hobbled? It was too hard to tell from this distance.

The cabin door opened, and Edward's muscles tightened down his back and shoulders. But instead of a man with bushy black hair and pale white skin, a little girl stepped out. She couldn't be more than five or six. Emmaline's age. His stomach clenched. Did Blackie have a daughter?

As he watched, the girl stopped to pet a cat that appeared from around the side of the cabin. Then she proceeded toward the edge of the yard where the tree line began. Was there a creek inside the woods where she fetched water? That seemed to be the case, because she reappeared moments later, her body tilting to one side under the weight of the full bucket.

After the child disappeared back inside the cabin, all fell silent in the clearing below. Minutes dragged on, but Edward and Townsend stayed motionless behind the rock. They had to get a better idea where Blackie was before they could put a plan together. The presence of the horse grazing in the distance seemed to indicate he was here. Unless he kept more than one horse. But the sorry condition of the meager dwelling made that seem unlikely. Of course, the man did have plenty of loot from his share of the bank robberies.

The door below opened again, and this time a woman appeared on the stoop. Her black hair glistened in the afternoon sun, and her tanned skin almost blended with the brown of her work dress. She carried something in her apron, and stopped at a stump about twenty feet from the cabin. Emptying her apron onto the stump's top surface, her hands moved back and forth over the items. But from this distance, it was impossible to see the details.

After a good five minutes of watching the woman work with her project, Edward turned to his partner and spoke in a whisper. "Maybe I should go down and talk to her. Say I'm passin' through and ask for a bite to eat. That might flesh out Blackie if he's inside, and you can cover from up here."

Townsend's grizzled face scrunched as he looked back at the scene below. Edward did the same, and waited a long minute before Townsend responded. The older man was a seasoned Ranger, with good instincts. And sometimes instincts took time to interpret.

"Might not be a bad plan. If we play it right. Could be better than waitin' up here all night." Another pause. "But I should be the one to go down. You're a better shot from this distance." His eyes crinkled a bit at the edges as he met Edward's gaze.

Edward glanced again at the scene below. He probably was the better sharpshooter. But could he send Townsend down into a possible trap? The woman working peacefully next to the stump didn't feel like an ambush. He sighed. "All right."

As his partner wove his horse down the hill, Edward kept his gun pointed toward the cabin. There was so much ground to cover down there. He scanned the area with both eyes. Townsend disappeared behind a copse of trees for a couple minutes at the bottom of the hill, and Edward's muscles drew up tighter, listening for any sound that might mean danger. Then the man reappeared at the edge of the yard.

The woman straightened from her work and turned to face him. The pitch of Townsend's voice drifted up to Edward, but the words were indefinable.

Suddenly, a blast rent the air. As if in slow motion, the Ranger pitched forward, then rolled to the ground. Edward frantically scanned the house, the yard, the tree line. Who fired the shot?

Then a movement through the trees grabbed his attention. A head of black hair darted between the leafless branches. Edward aimed his sights…and fired.

Chapter Eighteen

BETWEEN the branches below, Edward glimpsed the black-haired man's hands rise to his chest. Then he dropped to the ground.

Edward scanned the woods again. The yard. The cabin. Were there any others lying in ambush? No movements, aside from the slamming of the cabin door as the woman disappeared inside.

Was it safe to go down? Probably not, but he had to get to Townsend. The man writhed on the ground, clutching his shoulder. He may not last long without care. Edward needed to be down there.

He held his Winchester at the ready as he wound his way down the hill. Nearing the site where Blackie had fallen, Edward slowed. No movement appeared through the trees. He crept toward the body, lying face down among the decaying leaves. No movement there either. With a boot, he rolled the man over. A wide-eyed, glassy gaze stared up at him from a pale face. The man's thick black curls spoke of his Italian ancestry, while the almost white skin was said to have come from the Swedish relatives on his mother's side. Edward leaned down to touch the robber's neck. No blood thumped through his veins.

Straightening, he stared at the man, swallowing past the lump in his throat. No matter how many innocent people the skunk had threatened at gunpoint, he'd still had a mother and father who'd likely loved him.

A faint groan broke through the woods. Edward spun and crept toward the sound. As he pushed the branches aside and peered into the open yard, Edward's focus fell on Townsend, still lying prone on the ground. The dark-haired woman kneeled over him, pressing a cloth to his shoulder. Townsend groaned again and Edward stepped into the clearing, his rifle aimed toward the woman.

"Get back," he growled. He'd never had to point his gun at a woman before, but a fellow Ranger's life might be at stake.

Her dark eyes stared at him without fear, and she didn't move from her position by Townsend's shoulder. "He is much bleeding." She spoke with a heavy Spanish accent, but her words were understandable.

Edward sidled in a wide arc around them both, easing closer so he could see his friend. She lifted the cloth and peered at the exposed flesh of the man's shoulder. Somewhere along the way, his shirt had been opened to reveal the wound, likely at the hands of this woman.

"The bullet went in the back and came out here." She dabbed the blood that seeped out, so Edward could see the penny-size hole in the man's shoulder. Her explanation made sense.

She leaned back and rose to her feet, and Edward refocused the rifle's aim on her. The woman didn't acknowledge the gun, but instead, turned toward the house. "I will get whiskey to clean the wound." The words drifted over her shoulder as she marched to the cabin.

She had nerve, he'd give the woman that. How many rifles had been pointed at her in the past? He lowered his Winchester. But she'd been staying in Blackie's cabin. He couldn't afford to trust her yet, or he might end up like Townsend. On the ground with a bullet through his back.

Townsend groaned again. Edward stepped next to the man and crouched, but kept his gaze and rifle pointed toward the cabin. "You gonna make it?"

The Ranger gripped his wounded shoulder. "Hurts like fire."

"We'll get you bandaged, then head out of here to a doctor." Edward rested the gun across his legs, then quickly stripped first his jacket, then his shirt. It was the closest thing to a bandage he had.

Before he could get his coat back on, the cabin door opened, and the woman reappeared. She carried a clay jug in one hand and a stack of cloths in the other. He grabbed the rifle, scrambled to his feet, and stepped back. Wind whipped over his bare skin, leaving bumps across his flesh. He fought back a shiver.

The woman approached and dropped to her knees beside Townsend. "Put your shirt back on, Señor Ranger. I have cloths for bandage." She spoke without looking at him, but the disdain in her voice was clear. It made him want to duck his head, like a school boy who'd received a dressing down from his teacher. He squared his shoulders. He was a Texas Ranger, and didn't bow in shame to anyone in the state. But even as the thought stiffened his spine, he had the rifle in a grip between his knees and fumbled for the sleeves of his shirt.

"He has lost blood." The woman spoke as she peered under the bloody cloth over Townsend's wound. Then she uncorked the jug and slipped an arm under the man's head. "Drink. This will help with the pain."

The liquid seemed to do the trick, because Townsend gulped several times before pulling away. Setting the jug aside, the woman turned her wide dark eyes on Edward. "I will need your help to hold him while I clean the shoulder."

Edward hesitated. She seemed to be doing what was needed to help the man, but could he trust her enough to set the gun aside? Was she trying to disarm him for an attack? But surely he could overpower this small Mexican woman.

"I do not fight you, señor." Her words jerked his attention back to her face. "My husband was not a good man. He is dead now. I wish only to live peacefully here with mi hija." She spread her hand to take in the small cabin and the field where the animals grazed. "I will care for the wound. And then you and your amigo will go away. Sí?"

Her words seemed earnest. And even though her dark eyes were shadowed, there was a touch of pleading in them. This poor señora. How much had she been through with a good for nothing husband like Blackie?

Crouching on the other side of Townsend's body, he placed the rifle just behind his hip. "What should I do?"

"Hold his arms. This will burn, but will be better if he doesn't move."

Edward did as he was told, while the woman poured whiskey in the open wound. Townsend fought against Edward's hands on his shoulders, moaning as bloody bubbles oozed from the opening. The acrid odor of alcohol and blood scented the air. Edward gritted his teeth against the sight and the sounds. A burn rose from his stomach, but he swallowed it down.

The woman pressed a cloth against the wound and glanced up at Edward. "I need to do the same in the back."

Nodding, he rolled Townsend onto his stomach. The shirt stuck to his back in a viscous ring of crimson. The burn rose higher in Edward's throat, but he clamped his mouth against it.

The señora peeled the cloth back as she poured whiskey into the opening left by the bullet. This one was larger, closer to a half-dollar size. Townsend fought against the pain of the rancid liquid, but his efforts weren't as strong this time. His face had blanched almost white. *God, don't let me lose him.*

Within a few more seconds, the woman had clean cloths pressed in the wound, and a longer bandage positioned over Townsend's shoulder. They rolled him to his back again, and she tied the man's injured arm in a sling.

Edward pressed two fingers against his partner's neck, below his jaw. A steady beat thrummed there. Maybe they'd be able to leave today after all. He raised his gaze to the man's face and found him watching every movement.

"Jes get me to town where I can rest up a day. Then I'll be fine." Townsend's voice was weak, but at least he was coherent enough to make sense.

Turning to study Townsend's horse grazing at the edge of the yard, Edward scrambled for a plan. He needed to get them both back to town, along with Blackie's body.

And then another thought struck him. He looked over at the woman, Blackie's widow. "We need to take your husband's body back to town, ma'am. Would you and your daughter like to come with us?"

As he suspected, she shook her head. "No. Our place is here."

An unexpected lump stuck in his throat. Scanning the dusty yard, he swallowed. This place would be plenty of hard work for a strong man, much less a tiny woman and child.

"We've managed without help for years, Señor Ranger. It is no different now."

Had she read his mind? Edward turned to meet her gaze. The stubborn set of her jaw formed a stark contrast to the tired lines around her eyes. His chest squeezed. Something about her clutched at him, like an aching memory.

Alejandra had that same stubborn jaw when she first came to the ranch. And more than once, her eyes had glistened with the same pain and fear reflected in this woman's gaze.

The memory spurred an urgency within him. He had to see Alejandra.

He turned back to the woman. "Is there anything you need from your husband's body before I load up? Would you like to pay your respects?"

She shook her head.

"Can I help with anything here before we leave?" He scanned the yard. A pile of wood leaned against the wood frame of the cabin. At least they were stocked for a week or two. The place was in sad need of repair, but he couldn't spare time to reframe the building and patch the roof. Could he?

"Go, señor. Take your friend to the doctor." Her face was resigned, her eyes shimmering with sincerity. "We will be fine."

He released a breath. "All right."

After he hiked back up the hill to retrieve his horse, it took all his strength to lift Blackie's limp body onto Townsend's horse. Especially with the animal shifting away from the bulky form in his arms. Getting Townsend on Edward's own mount was only slightly easier. The man broke out in a sweat with the effort, his skin almost as pale as Blackie's.

"Stay with me, partner." Edward swung up behind the man, then reached for the reins to the other horse the señora held for him.

"You want to take whiskey for him?" She nodded toward Townsend as he doubled over the saddle horn.

Should he? It should only take a few hours to reach town, and how much could a few occasional sips help the man? "No. Gracias."

The little girl crept up behind her mother, and the woman stepped back to join her.

He couldn't help but stare at the two of them. The little girl, so much like Emmaline. And the brave young mother, so much like Alejandra. And now they were completely alone. Widowed and fatherless.

And he'd been the one to make them that way. The thought smashed into him like a blow to his lungs. Anger sluiced through him. Fury at Blackie, for being the despicable skunk he'd been. And at himself, for leaving these women alone and helpless. Sure he'd been doing his job, killing the desperado. But had he ever done anything to help the family members left abandoned by the blood shed at his own hands?

Why did he do this job? To help people? That was what he told himself. But was that really what drove him every day? Or was it the need to prove himself? But at what cost? Alejandra wouldn't come near him as long as he wore the badge. Was it really worth it?

The country needed Rangers like Townsend. Men who could handle the rough parts. Even take a bullet and keep fighting against the lawless. But he was tired of putting his life on the line every day for a selfish goal. Tired of leaving his family, sometimes for weeks at a time. And he wanted Alejandra to trust him.

Nodding in farewell to the woman and child, Edward nudged his horse forward. Once he dropped these men at the first town, he was headed to Headquarters in Austin to resign his commission. His Rangering days were over.

Chapter Nineteen

EDWARD pushed open the door to Headquarters, removing his hat as he entered. He strode toward the simple desk that stood like a guard in front of the corridor to the offices.

Nodding to the man with the handle-bar mustache who sat behind it, he asked. "Captain Peak in his office?"

The man reached for the pocket watch at the top of his vest pocket. "Yes, but he has an appointment in five minutes."

"I shouldn't need longer than that." Edward skirted the desk and strode down the hall to the second door on the right. Before he could knock, it swung open.

Captain Peak lifted a brow at Edward's raised hand, but stepped aside and swept a hand for Edward to enter. "Come in, Stewart. I was just about to wire you. I need you to lead a company of Rangers to bring in the Garza gang."

"The Garza gang, sir?"

The captain paced as he spoke. "We think there are seven or eight in the group, and they've been terrorizing the country

189

from Nuevo Laredo almost to San Antonio. They've robbed two stages, killed all the passengers, and burned at least a dozen homesteads, torturing the families before they killed them." The man whirled and leveled his gaze on Edward. "They have to be stopped, Stewart. And I think you're the man to lead the mission. Are you up for it?"

Edward swallowed. Lead this assignment? He was here to resign. But how could he say no when so many lives were at stake? If this gang wasn't stopped, how many more innocent families would be tortured and murdered?

"I'll make you an acting Sergeant for this assignment. And if it's successful—which I'm sure it will be…" Captain Peak sent him a pointed look. "I should be able to get my recommendation passed to promote you to Sergeant permanently. You'll have earned it."

The Captain spun and marched to his desk, as if the matter were settled. "Here's the poster for the gang. And the notes on their known attacks. You'll have five Rangers with you. Meet them at the jail in San Antonio no later than tomorrow morning." He held several papers in Edward's direction.

Should he speak what he'd come to say? Or take this assignment and deal with the resignation later?

When the papers weren't immediately taken, Peak's brows lowered. "What's wrong?"

The question was enough to spur Edward into action. "Sir. I came here to resign my commission. I'll take this last assignment, if you need me to. But then, I'll have to bow out. It's been a pleasure to serve under you though, Captain."

Captain Peak stroked a hand over the course gray hair of his beard. "I'm sorry to hear that, Stewart. You plannin' to settle down?"

Edward met the man's softened gaze. "Maybe so."

The captain stepped around the desk, and clapped Edward on the back as he handed him the papers. "I hope she's worth it, son. The Rangers will miss you."

TWO days later, Edward stretched out on his saddle blanket under a cloudy night sky, weariness weighting his bones. His muscles were conditioned to jostling in the saddle all day, but with this assignment on the heels of tracking down Blackie...his endurance was wearing thin.

They'd covered some good ground today. But after inspecting the burnt shells of the houses the Garza gang had torched, and seeing all those fresh graves—his muscles had formed hard knots along his shoulders. And it didn't help that the gang's trail looked to be along the route just north of Seguin. Was his family in danger? The Double Rocking B was on the south side of town. And two miles out. Surely that meant they were safe.

Pulling his bedroll blanket a little higher on his chest, Edward allowed his eyelids to drift shut. As he inhaled several deep breaths, the night sounds crept into his awareness. Crickets. An owl hooting to its mate. This would be a nice evening to sit on the front porch at the Double Rocking B and enjoy the animal noises. With Alejandra beside him.

The familiar pang tightened his chest. She permeated every thought, every action. What would she say about his change of vocation? The thought almost pushed him upright. What would he do for a living now? Go back to work for Jacob? In some subconscious region of his mind, that's what he must have been planning. But was that really what he wanted?

God, what's your plan for me? He tried to still himself. Quiet his racing thoughts and listen for his Father's voice. A fragment from Scripture flitted through his mind. *Seek ye first the kingdom of God.* It was a passage he'd read yesterday morning over a breakfast of dried jerky and coffee.

Edward rose from his makeshift bed, careful not to disturb the other Rangers stretched out around the campfire. He reached for the leather-bound Bible from his saddle bag, and flipped to the book of Matthew, chapter six.

Therefore take no thought, saying, What shall we eat? Or, What shall we drink? Or, Wherewithal shall we be clothed?
For after all these things the Gentiles seek, but your heavenly Father knoweth that ye have need of all these things.

But seek ye first the kingdom of God, and His righteousness; and all these things shall be added unto you.

Take therefore no thought for the morrow; for the morrow shall take thought for the things of itself. Sufficient unto the day is the evil thereof.

Edward drew in a long breath, then released it, letting go of the tension in his muscles. *Okay, God. You're right. I have a job to do now. But I need You to keep my family safe. And Alejandra. Give me strength to deal with the evil I'll be facing.*

ALEJANDRA reined the Palomino mare down to a walk as they entered the stretch of woods that bordered the Guadalupe River. She owed Mama Sarita a debt for taking care of breakfast this morning. But with the faint traces of morning fog still swirling around her, and the chill invigorating her senses, it was all worth the chance to escape for an early morning excursion to the river. She pulled the cloak tighter around her.

When she arrived at the water, she tied the mare to the large live oak at the river's edge. After removing the cloak from her shoulders, she placed it on a large rock, then sat atop it to soak up the morning sun as it glinted off the blue water. She'd been here a few times since Edward first showed her the spot, but none compared to that first trip with him.

What was it about Edward's presence that made the little things come alive for her? He was a mystery. Despite everything she'd learned to associate with men that wore a badge, Edward was different. He'd proven his kindness so many times. And not just kindness to her—but also to Anna, little Emmaline, the tiny niño, Mama Sarita. Even the care and concern he'd given the little runt puppy, Sol. All the vaqueros seemed to respect him.

Did that mean she could trust Edward, too? Bumps raised on the back of her arms. Could she trust a man who wore a badge? What if he hurt her like the other soldiers had? Only this time, if the longing in her chest meant anything, it would be her heart left scarred, not her face.

A horse nickered softly behind her. She turned toward the sound, but a hand clamped over her mouth, jerking her head back. What in the world? Fear shot through her.

Before she could get her bearings, another arm gripped her waist in a vice, holding her arms tight to her sides. As the hands dragged her backward off the rock, she fought to scream, but the sound strangled in her throat.

And then she was surrounded. Men everywhere. Dark-skinned Mexican men. Binding her hands in front of her, stuffing a filthy rag into her mouth and tying it tight. They held her feet so she couldn't kick out, while one after another leered in front of her. Touching her cheeks, her neck. One man ran a hand all the way down her side, saying things more vile than she'd thought possible. *Oh, God. Don't let them do such things!*

Without warning, she was jerked off her feet, and hauled like a limp sack draped over a man's arm. The muscled hold across her body and the gag sealing off her mouth brought back a wash of memories. Nightmares she'd fought against for years. The last time she'd been bound like a criminal and carried by a rough soldier...the most awful day of her life. Would this experience be even worse?

Dangling in this precarious position over the man's arm, her legs were free. She used the opportunity to its full extent, striking hard with her boots into any flesh she could reach.

The man swore. Suddenly, she was flying through the air, tossed like a tortilla over his shoulder, her legs clamped together under the man's arm. She couldn't move now. Could barely breathe with the weight of her body pushing down on her chest against the desperado's back, and the rag over her mouth.

After a few more jouncing strides, she was hoisted away from him and tossed up into a saddle. She landed hard on the leather-wrapped horn, searing lightning bolts shooting through her body. Again an arm clamped around her midsection, as the man in the saddle behind her held tight. Alejandra fought to lean forward, pulling her body as far away from his as she could.

"What's the matter, querida?" That leering voice. It had to be the same man who'd spoken the awful things a moment ago. He tightened his hold, pressing her body against his.

Alejandra stopped fighting, dread pricking her skin. She kept her body as rigid as possible. The hot, foul-smelling breath on her neck made her stomach roil, threatening to bring up the corn atole she ate before leaving the house.

The other men mounted horses, and a tall skinny one motioned toward the trees up river. The rest fell into line behind him, weaving through the trees at a fast walk, sometimes breaking into a trot when the foliage wasn't as dense. The chill of the morning was worse in the woods, and Alejandra fought against the shivers that threatened. Why had she taken her cloak off? There were three riders ahead of her, and she'd only gotten a glimpse of the others, but maybe two or three behind.

They rode through the woods for what seemed hours, branches smacking Alejandra's face and arms when the riders ahead pulled them back. One particular whack on her jaw stung longer than the others, and a trickle of moisture itched as it crawled down her face. With her hands bound, the best she could do was wipe it against her shoulder, leaving a large red smear on her beige shirtwaist.

At last, they broke through the edge of the woods and turned onto a road. The man in the front called "Cisco!" and the horse just ahead of Alejandra left the line and trotted up to the leader. The men shared a few terse comments, then Cisco spurred his horse and took off ahead of them at a canter.

The men settled into a quiet line again, the horses clomping at a steady trot on the narrow road. With the mid-morning sun shining down, Alejandra finally began to thaw. She craned her neck both directions, trying to find a landmark

The Ranger Takes a Bride

that might place their surroundings. Only trees lined both sides of the road. It wasn't a path she'd ridden before. Were they moving away from Seguin? Surely if they were headed toward the town, they would have been there by now. So were they riding toward San Antonio? Moving upriver meant they were going north, right? But she hadn't seen the river since they first captured her, so she really had no idea which way they were headed.

About an hour later, a shrill whistle pierced the air, and then the leader motioned toward the trees on their right side. The group merged into the woods, weaving away from the road for a minute or two before the leader barked an order, and they reined their horses back in a single file line. They seemed to be riding in the same direction as the road now, so why had they left it? The whistle must have been a sign from the scout sent ahead. Did that mean other travelers were headed her direction? Alejandra's heartbeat sped at the thought, desperation driving it harder. They were far enough from the road that any faint noise she made through the gag would never be heard. And she couldn't risk angering these men until she had a plausible opportunity for escape. She'd have to keep her eyes open—somehow come up with a plan.

As if he could read her mind, the man's burly arm around Alejandra's waist tightened. The gravelly voice spoke in her ear. "Don't even think about it, Senorita. You are mine until I am through with you." His thumb sneaked up to stroke the swell of her side. She tensed, jerking away from his touch. He chuckled before sliding his hand back to her waist.

An icy prickle shot down Alejandra's spine. She had to find a way of escape.

Chapter Twenty

THEY didn't stop for lunch, but rode for hour after long hour. Sometimes on the road, sometimes through the forest. Hunger gnawed at Alejandra. It had been a long time since that simple mug of atole before dawn. Her stomach let out a loud growl, and she felt her jailor shift behind her. He pulled a fistful of thick jerky slices from his saddle bag. With a yank that almost snapped her neck, he pulled the gag out of her mouth so it hung loose above her shirt collar. She couldn't stop a moan as her bound hands crept up to touch the raw skin around her lips.

He pushed a chunk of meat into her hand, and Alejandra scrambled to catch it. If it fell to the ground, he probably wouldn't stop to pick it up…or give her a second piece. The man ripped off a bite of another with his teeth. He chomped like a cow chewing corn, smacking his gums in a way that grated on her nerves.

She stared at the piece of dark beef in her hand. The thought of eating food from the hand of these foul men took away her hunger, especially with the noises emanating from the rude bull behind her. But she had to keep up her strength if she was to have any thought of escaping. And who knew when she would have another chance to eat? The sun had crested the peak of the sky a while back. Would they stop for dinner tonight? Surely these men would take time to fill their own bellies.

Eyeing the meat again, she bit off a corner. Or tried to. It was more salt than anything, but she had to saw the hardtack back and forth a few times before her teeth finally broke through. She didn't hurry through the "meal," but after a few bites her stomach remembered its hunger. She fought the urge to scarf down the rest, forcing herself to chew every bite fully. If nothing else, it gave her something to do while time passed, and kept him from putting the gag back in place. The moment she put the last piece in her mouth though, the desperado behind her yanked the dirty cloth back over her chin.

"Oh…" Alejandra couldn't help the sound that escaped as he scraped his claws over the skin on her face, compressing her jaw bones with his rough efforts. At last, he must have been satisfied with the gag, because his hand trailed back down to her waist, lingering over everything it touched on the way down. Alejandra's entire body tensed, the pain on her face erased by the burn of his touch. Rage coursed through her veins, and it took every bit of self-control to keep herself from wrenching out of his arms. He seemed to sense it, for his hand settled around her midsection again, his grip tightening at her side. She'd never escape through a struggle. The only way out would be through outsmarting these despicable men.

What was happening back at the ranch? How long had it taken before they'd missed her? Mama Sarita had told her to spend the morning at the river, so it may be after lunch before someone came to look for her. Did that mean they might just now be finding her horse tied to the tree? Would they suspect she'd been kidnapped? Or think she'd gone for a walk and gotten lost, or maybe fallen into the river? A weight settled over Alejandra as she realized how many possible scenarios they might imagine for her disappearance. What were the odds of them realizing what had really happened, and tracking this band of desperados over these many miles? The likelihood was almost non-existent. Alejandra inhaled a breath. If she had any chance of survival or escape, it was up to her.

The sun was hidden behind the trees on the far horizon when they left the road again and split off into a trail through the woods. There had been no whistle this time to signal an oncoming traveler. Were they preparing to make camp?

She watched for signs of their destination, and the trail finally opened into a small clearing where a little shack huddled in the center. The man called Cisco had already dismounted beside a hitching rail and lifted the saddle from his horse's back as the rest of them filed into the open area.

The man holding Alejandra dismounted, sliding her down with him. She scrambled to catch her footing, but her feet had gone numb hours ago from the horn poking into her legs. Now, they were useless. Fear washed through her as she sank to her knees. But her captor seized her arm and jerked her upright. *Come on, feet. Move.*

Tossing his reins to another outlaw, he half-drug half-carried her toward the shack, her limp feet dragging the ground and tangling in her full skirts. The man shouldered the door open, then jerked to a stop at the threshold. Alejandra tried again to gather her feet under her. They were coming alive now, shooting prickles of pain through both legs.

The man strode forward again, dragging her with him. Alejandra scrambled, and this time was able to limp along beside him. Stopping in front of a round heating stove, he pushed her to the ground beside it, her dirty brown skirt billowing around her. Was the metal of the stove hot? She scooted away from it.

"Sit down," he growled.

He extracted a rope from his pocket, yanked her skirt aside to reveal the skin just above her boots, then tied her legs together. The rough leather cord bit into her still-stinging skin, and she had to grip her lip between her teeth to keep from crying out. After knotting the rope tight, he pulled her legs close to the iron leg of the stove. Alejandra shrank back, preparing herself for the searing heat from the iron. Her flesh met cool metal, and she almost wilted in relief.

With a jerk, the man grabbed the rope that bound her wrists and peered at it, pulling it close to his face as he squinted. Did he see any marks? She'd fumbled with the cord some while they rode, but couldn't get her finger anywhere near the knot. He fiddled with the tie, his beady eyes roaming from the leather to her face, then back to the leather.

At last, he threw down the rope, jerking her hands in the process. "You be a good girl, querida. Sì? After holding you all day, it won't be long before I come back to claim you as mine." His snicker sent a shiver through her. He cupped her cheek and ended her torment with a pinch before he rose to his feet.

As he strode out the door, her shoulders sagged for the first time since her capture. She'd refused to let them read defeat in her posture, but nobody watched now. She scanned the room, her eyes taking in every feature. The only light that filtered in came through a greased-paper window near the front door. Stark walls and dirt floor. Just like the shanty she and Papa had shared at Rancho Las Cuevas. Except this room held none of the homey warmth she'd worked so hard to create there. A cook stove sat in the far corner, with two shelves hanging on the wall near it. On the back wall beside her, a rear door was held shut by a simple leather tie strap. In the center of the room, a long table dominated, with six mismatched chairs around it. Aside from the heating stove she was tied to, no other furniture filled the small space. Nothing that promised escape.

If she could somehow free her hands and legs, maybe she could hit the men with the frying pan on the stove. The chairs didn't look sturdy enough to do much damage. But how to get rid of the leather binding her wrists? Alejandra worked the strap up and down over the smooth metal of the stove leg. Maybe if she rubbed it long enough, she could wear the strap thin so it would break.

But after several minutes of forceful scraping, the leather didn't look any thinner, and her wrists wore angry red lines from the effort. The front door flew open, banging against the wall. Alejandra jerked away from the stove, and shrank back into the shadows as three outlaws poured into the room.

The youngest of them grabbed a tin bucket from beside the cook stove, then left the cabin again. A chunky man pulled a canister from a shelf and set to work dumping ingredients into some of the pans on the stove. The third man, the oldest in the group if the salt flecks in his hair spoke true, carried an armload of logs, and proceeded to build a fire in the cook stove. The chunky man barked a few indecipherable words at his partner—probably trying to speed up the fire-making, as the men worked practically on top of each other—but the *anciano* just grunted.

Neither of them spared a glance at Alejandra. Maybe she could keep trying to rub through the rope at her hands. Shifting her body slightly so it blocked her actions from their view, she sawed up and down on the metal surface. When the older man slammed the stove door shut, Alejandra jumped.

As he disappeared out the front door, the youngest man came in carrying the bucket—full of water it appeared. Her captors kept up a steady stream in and out of the cabin for the next several minutes. Each time someone passed by her, Alejandra stopped sawing the leather rope and tried her best to melt into the metal of the stove she was tied to. The way their eyes roamed over her body, it was as if they looked right through her clothing, leaving her dirty and defiled.

The chunky man at the stove was the only one who ignored her. An aroma drifted into Alejandra's awareness while she sawed at the leather. Coffee. And corn. Was he making atole? Or cornbread? Corn tortillas? Her stomach rumbled as her mind churned. She had to stop thinking about food, or she would drive herself loco.

Chunky pushed the frying pan to the back burner on the stove, then wiped a hand on his pants leg and strode out the door.

Alejandra stopped rubbing the rope long enough to examine the leather at her hands. There was barely a hint of a shiny spot on the coarse surface. Her heart plummeted. At this rate, it might take all night to rub through the leather. And the knot in her stomach reminded her she wouldn't be tied here when night fell. These desperados had plans for her. Awful plans.

Panic welled in Alejandra's chest, like a wild animal clawing to escape. She would be ravaged by these men. And then, quite likely murdered. If she were lucky. Was this the way God intended it? Had he brought her this far only to let her be molested and killed by these savages?

Sometimes things happen that don't make sense, and it's hard to believe God can love us and still let those things happen.

Anna's words from before Navidad came back like a thought spoken in her mind. What had she said next?

But God has a plan...to give you a hope and a future.

A hope and a future? From where Alejandra sat now, her future looked pretty dim. Could God really save her from this? Did she dare ask him to help? After all the years she'd nurtured bitterness and anger toward God, would He listen to her at all?

Alejandra inhaled a shaky breath. *God, if You're listening, and if You care...I'm in trouble here. If you don't hate me...please, save me?*

She sat very still waiting for a sign. Something to show her prayer had made it up to God's ears. Something to prove He listened. Or cared.

But, Alejandra... Anna's words again, as clear as if her friend were sitting beside her in this barren shack ...*moving forward into that future requires forgiving God for the past.*

The knot tightened in Alejandra's stomach. Forgive God? For her mother's murder? For the terrible things that happened to them both? For letting Papa die? For stripping her of everything and everyone she loved?

Like images of scenery flying by from the back of a racing horse, visions flashed through her mind. Edward. Mama Sarita. Anna. Emmaline. One after another, they paraded. Appearing and disappearing in her memory's eye. She had so many good people in her life now. People she'd come to care deeply about. Was life at the O'Brien ranch the hope and future God had given her? And would He now take it away?

...*moving forward into that future requires forgiving God for the past.*

Forgive God. Could she really forgive God for her past? Alejandra drew her knees up in front of her and dropped her forehead to rest on them. This rock of bitterness in her heart had grown so large, the ache of it radiated through her body. She was tired of fighting. Tired of hating. Tired of trying to control. Tired of running. *God, I'm sorry. I don't know what's right anymore. I've blamed You for all the bad. I don't understand it, but I'm tired of hating You. Can You forgive me? Will You help me? I want that hope and future Anna says You have for me. And I want to be on Your side.*

An overwhelming peace washed through Alejandra like rain, leaving behind a clean that started from the inside and worked its way out. Gone was the violated feeling left by the outlaws' stares. Gone was the fear that had dogged every step since she was twelve years old. Only a stillness in her soul. A lightness like she'd never experienced. A joy she wanted to hold onto.

Chapter Twenty-One

SHE didn't have long to enjoy the peaceful feeling, because the front door crashed open again, and all six men tromped in. After tossing aside hats and coats, they each grabbed a plate and mug from a shelf, filled them from pans at the stove, and settled into the rickety chairs around the table.

All except one man, who pulled his chair close to the lone window. The meager light that eked through the dirty paper illuminated skin so dark it almost matched the black of his hair. She could just see the tip of a rifle barrel that rested across his lap. Did they think someone followed them? Or did the group always live in fear of being discovered, even in this remote hideout?

As the men ate with grunts and slurping sounds, Alejandra's stomach rumbled again. She pressed her arm into it. The last thing she wanted was to draw these outlaws' attention to herself. But the vulgar man whom she'd ridden with all day stopped eating and eyed her, a twisted smile parting his mouth. "Hungry, querida?" But he didn't make a move to feed her, only raised his mug to his lips and gulped. He never stopped watching her, though, and the gleam in his eye raised bumps on her arms.

Alejandra hunkered into as much of a ball as she could with her legs tied to the stove and her wrists bound together. *God, I'm trusting you, but this is hard.*

The meal lasted for hours. At least it felt like it did. With all these men in the shack, the room seemed to shrink until there was no air left to breathe. Just evil that filled the void, pressing into her pores, trying to steal away her new peace.

God, I'm trusting you. She spoke it like a mantra in her mind. Over and over, so she didn't have to look at these vile men. Didn't have to think about what they had planned next. She'd take good soldiers like Edward any day instead of banditos malvados like these.

Edward. An ache pierced her soul. Would she ever see him again?

Suddenly, a crash split the air as the door beside Alejandra exploded inward. Chairs flew backward as the desperados around the table jumped to their feet. Gunshots exploded in the air, and men swarmed the room. Bodies fell to the ground. Some lay still, others grappled in pairs with fists flying. She glimpsed silver on one man's chest. Soldiers. *Gracias, Dio!*

A man crashed to the ground right in front of Alejandra. His familiar face was turned to her, eyes rolled back in his head. That man. The vile one who'd promised to do all those wicked things to her. A breath of relief escaped her lips, even as she scrambled as far away from his lifeless body as her bonds would allow. She tucked her face into her shoulder as chaos took over around her.

God had sent help, but would she survive the bullets whizzing around her?

EDWARD blinked at the sight of the woman huddled by the stove. But a blow slammed into his shoulder, and he spun to face the assault. A dark-skinned man must have been thrown into him, and now picked himself up like a bull, ready to charge again. In two strides, Edward grabbed the man's arms, and spun him around so they were crossed behind him. The hombre struggled, but he was a young, skinny fellow and looked like he might have had the sense knocked out of him before he was thrown into Edward.

Dragging him out, Edward handed him over to Parker, who was watching two of their other prisoners at the edge of the yard. Another shot sounded inside the cabin, and Edward sprinted back in. From his first count, there should only be three outlaws left inside, and he'd seen one of them fall dead in front of the woman captive. A lump settled in his stomach. Had they arrived soon enough to save her from real harm? She'd been curled in a ball, but the glimpse he'd caught of her rich black hair brought out that ache in his chest for Alejandra. He couldn't think about her now. No distractions.

He peeked around the doorway before entering, so he could get the positions of his men and the outlaws. Every Ranger who valued his life knew better than to charge into a room where bullets were flying. McLellan was tying the hands of a stout Mexican who was giving him an ear-full, and Cap bent over the body of a tall, lanky man. That had to be Garza. According to the Wanted poster, the man was "six feet, one inch and of lean stature." Other than the kid, this man was the only one who could pass for lean.

Edward turned his attention to the woman by the stove, still curled in a ball with her head tucked into her shoulder. Stepping to her side, he gentled his voice. "Ma'am. Everything's okay now. We're Texas Rangers, and those outlaws..."

She turned to face him, and Edward's words froze. His brain refused to process what his eyes took in.

Those wide eyes, so dark and expressive. That face, every delicate feature. Now dirty and disheveled.

Alejandra.

She was gagged and bound, but a sound leaked through the thick cloth in her mouth. Was that his name?

He dropped to his knees and gathered her in his arms. "Alejandra. How?"

She burrowed in his chest, her warmth flooding him with a torrent of emotion. How did she get here? She was supposed to be safe at the ranch.

"Alejandra." He breathed in her scent.

She squirmed, and he pulled back a few inches. The rag tied around her mouth spurred him into action.

"I'm sorry." He whispered the words while he eased his knife under the fabric at the back of her head. She cringed when the blade pulled the cloth tighter.

With the gag off, he made short work of the rope that bound her hands, then the strap above her boots. The angry marks where the coarse leather had dug in sent a fresh spurt of anger through his veins. He'd see every one of those low-lives hang.

The moment Alejandra was freed, she turned to face Edward and catapulted into his arms. The force almost knocked him backward, but he caught himself, and folded her in his body. So tight.

Oh, God. Thank You. She's alive. But how did she get here? What had they done to her? He'd get those answers soon.

But for now, nothing mattered more than holding her. Alejandra. How was it possible to love this much?

ALEJANDRA pressed deeper into Edward's embrace. With every breath, she inhaled him. His strength. His security. Resting her head against his chest, she settled into the steady drum of his heartbeat. He was here. He'd saved her.

Or rather, God saved her. *Gracias, Dio. Muchas gracious.*

A smile pulled at Alejandra's mouth, and she snuggled deeper into Edward's hug. Her eyes drifted closed.

He tightened his hold, and the soft touch of his lips caressed the top of her head. "Alejandra." His whisper was the sweetest sound she'd ever heard.

Before she was ready, he loosened his grip and leaned back to look at her. With his free hand, he lifted her chin so he could see her face. The gentlest of touches. "What happened? How did you get here?"

The question brought back the whole awful ordeal in a frightening blur. She bit her lower lip to stop it from trembling. Here in Edward's arms, with God on her side, she was safe. "I went to the river this morning, and they found me there. They tied me so I couldn't run or cry for help. We rode all day until we reached this place."

"Did they...hurt you?" Edward's voice thickened so much the last words seemed to strangle him as they escaped.

Alejandra swallowed, her eyes dropping to the buttons marching down his shirt. For a moment, her heart relived the filth of their stares, and bumps rose on her arms. "If you had not come, I..." Her words were barely more than a whisper.

Edward's hand slid from her chin to her cheek, cradling it in the warmth of his work-roughened fingers. Her gaze wandered up to his, and the emotion there was her undoing. Those brown eyes pooled with concern. Moisture rose into her own eyes, stinging her throat as it traveled up. She nibbled her lip to keep the liquid at bay, but a single tear broke through her barrier.

Edward's thumb swept it away, and he lowered his forehead so it rested on hers. "I will never let them hurt you again." His words were a breathy whisper. A fervent promise. His chest vibrated with each passionate sound.

His head came lower, and his mouth claimed hers. Sealing the promise he'd spoken. His touch was warm. Soft. Strong. So richly sweet.

Alejandra was lost from the moment he touched her. His kiss took away every thought, every awareness. Everything...but him. When Edward pulled away, her mouth almost followed him. She blinked, her gaze finding his again. Those chocolate eyes were dark with intensity. The emotion there matched what stirred her own soul. A smile tugged at one corner of her mouth. "I've never been so happy to see a soldado."

He blinked, then his gaze searched hers. He must have liked what he found there, because his own mouth curved upward. "I'm glad. You know, it was God that brought me to you."

Alejandra swallowed, that same peace flooding her veins again. "I know. I prayed, Edward. Told Him I wanted His help to forgive. I trusted Him." Tears burned her eyes again, as the enormity of what happened struck her. She'd trusted God to save her, and He had. The ordeal was over, and she had little more than a few rope burns. Joy erupted in her chest, flooding every inch of her body.

Edward's face matched her soul, moisture lighting his brown eyes. "I'm glad," he said again, pulling her to his chest in a fervent embrace. "So glad."

A knock at the open door interrupted the hug. Edward pulled back, stroking her cheek with the pad of his thumb, apology in his eyes. "I need to speak with my men, then we'll go home." He held her gaze a final moment, and something in his look promised they would finish this conversation later.

"Sì. All right."

He helped her stand, never removing his arm from around her waist. Alejandra leaned into him, especially when her feet didn't seem to work. As she scanned the room, it was empty. Where had all the men gone?

Edward turned toward the back door. A man with a Ranger star on his chest stood there, hands behind his back and head bent down to watch his feet scuff the ground. The man's cheeks had a red flush to them.

He cleared his throat. "Sorry to, uh…disturb you, Sarge." The man finally looked up at Edward. "We got 'em all tied. There's one dead, but the rest are either healthy or just banged up. Garza's fit as a house cat. We takin' 'em to Austin?"

"Yep. That's the closest jail with good security, and they've got a regular judge. These rats are gonna hang." His grip tightened around Alejandra's side, and she could feel the steel lacing his voice.

"All right." The other Ranger nodded, then shot a quick glance at Alejandra before looking back at Edward. "You, uh…gonna look after the captive?"

The tight muscles in Edward's arm softened, and his chest reverberated behind Alejandra's shoulder as he chuckled. "As long as I live, Lord willing. McLellan, I'd like you to meet Miss Diaz. She's been working on my sister's ranch." The steel reentered his voice. "I had no idea she was here until I saw her tied to that stove."

McLellan raised his brows. "Probably a good thing you didn't know."

Edward acknowledged the comment with a terse nod. "If you think you guys can handle the prisoners, I'll take Alejandra home."

McLellan clapped Edward on the shoulder. "We'll see to it, Sarge."

When the man strode out of the doorway, Edward turned back to Alejandra. His dark eyes softened, caressing her face. "It's going to be dark soon. The closest town is over an hour away. Think you can make it that far?"

Get back on another horse? Weariness settled into Alejandra's bones at the thought. But she could do this. She had to. Staying here was not an option.

But when she met Edward's concerned gaze, it wasn't hard to summon a smile. "I can make it."

His eyes creased at the corners. He pulled her close and planted a kiss on her forehead that started a longing in her chest. She almost grabbed his shirt collar and pulled him down for a real kiss, but settled with resting her hands on his chest. His heartbeat was strong under her palms.

Loosening his grip around her waist, Edward reached up to take her hand. "Come on." His voice was thick, gravelly. "My horse is this way." He stood motionless for another moment, as if he couldn't quite force himself to move. Then he turned and led the way outside. His grip on her hand never wavered.

Pepper waited with the other Rangers' horses at the edge of the clearing. Each of the outlaws were already mounted on their own animals. Her hold on Edward's hand tightened as she scanned their faces. The chunky man who'd cooked. The younger one who wasn't much more than a boy. The awful man with the vile tongue lay draped over his horse. Dead. She fought down a shiver, as Edward's thumb stroked the top of her hand.

Chapter Twenty-Two

ALEJANDRA gripped Edward's hand as he led her straight to Pepper. After Edward mounted, the Ranger named McLellan moved toward Alejandra. She shifted away from him, pressing into Edward's leg and the horse's side. Even though these men had just helped her. Saved her life. The instinct to flee from any man with a soldier's badge would be hard to overcome.

"It's all right, love. He's going to help you up on Pepper." Edward's voice was quiet enough for her ears alone to hear.

Inhaling a deep breath, she allowed the man to help her mount behind Edward. Wrapping her arms around his waist, she snuggled in close, absorbing his heat and security. Edward's hand held hers firmly in place.

They started out at a walk, following behind the rest of the men as they wound through the woods. When they reached the road, the others turned left, but Edward reined his horse to the right. Toward home. And what a story she would have to tell.

"You up for a slow canter?" Edward's voice rumbled against her cheek as she pressed her face to his back.

She sat up straighter to speak into his ear, lest her voice be carried away by the wind. "Sì."

Pepper struck out into a rolling lope, and she tightened her grip around Edward as she tried to settle into the rocking motion. The horse was smoother than most, but she had the feeling if she didn't hang on tight, she would float right off the back.

A few minutes later, Edward slowed the gelding to a walk. Relief washed over Alejandra as her muscles relaxed. Her stomach took that opportunity to release a loud grumble. Heat flooded up her neck and into her face.

Edward twisted to look at her, and she caught the lines furrowing his forehead. "I'm sorry. I didn't think about whether you'd eaten. There's some jerky in that saddle bag behind you. Might be a peppermint stick, too."

She opened the flap where he pointed, and found the canvas bag she usually packed with food for him to take on assignments. The familiar sight sent a twinge through her chest. She'd be home soon. Inside were two slices of dried meat and a single white stick-like object. Was this all the food he'd planned to eat tonight? It wouldn't be enough for them both.

She held the meager supplies in her palm for him to take, but he closed her hand over the food, pushing it away. "They're for you. I've had about all the jerky I can stomach over the last week." He rubbed his flat midsection as he spoke.

Her stomach ached, and the threat of another loud noise kept her from protesting. "Gracias." Within minutes, the meat was gone. She held up the white stick, examining it in the fading light. She'd never seen anything like it, but she'd heard peppermint sticks were a kind of sweet candy. Edward would enjoy it later. Tucking it back in the canvas sack, she nestled the material in the saddle bag, then buckled the latch and slipped her arms back around Edward. Snuggled against him like this, she could ride all night.

"ALEJANDRA, love. It's time to wake up."

The soft pillow beneath Alejandra's head shifted, and she clutched tighter to hold it in place.

"Alejandra."

That voice. It flowed over her like warm honey. Soothing and sweet. The pillow shifted under her cheek, and strong arms tightened around her. A familiar scent filled her nostrils, a mixture of man and nature.

Alejandra forced her eyes open, just as something soft and a little warm touched her forehead. She blinked. Then drew back. Edward sat beside her. A rakish grin touched the side of his mouth as he watched her.

She looked around, trying to sort through the fog in her brain. She sat…on a horse?

Then it all rushed back. The outlaws. Edward saving her. They'd been riding. Heat flamed into her face. She must have fallen asleep.

He slid from the animal's back, and she glanced around again. They were in some kind of building, with a wide open door to her back, and a hard-packed dirt floor littered with hay. Edward reached to help her down, and Alejandra complied.

"I've got a stall ready for the gelding." A baritone voice drifted from the shadows, loud and commanding.

She startled, and Edward slipped a hand around her back. "Thanks, Simon. I'll be back for him in the morning." Edward's tone was strong and steady, which helped settle the rapid beat in her chest.

He untied his saddle bags and the sling that held his rifle, then gripped Alejandra's elbow and escorted her toward the open doorway. "You think you can eat before we call it a night?"

Alejandra jerked her gaze to his face. They were going to sleep here? Where? Surely he didn't mean anything indecent.

A hint of a grin touched his face. "There's a hotel just across the street. I'm sure they'll have a couple rooms open for us."

A hotel? A trickle of unease tightened her stomach. She'd never stayed in a hotel before. They cost too much. Were they so far from home they couldn't make it tonight? But he was probably exhausted, too. He'd been away from the ranch for almost a week now.

With an exhale, Alejandra resigned herself to follow Edward's lead, and soon they entered a large room with several

221

square tables surrounded by chairs. The aromas that wafted through the air started her middle rumbling again. She pressed a hand to her waist to keep it from growing louder.

"Ya'll sit anywhere you like." A lady with dark ebony skin flashed them a perky smile as she filled mugs for a group of four men.

Edward guided Alejandra to a table in the corner. She reached for a seat, but he tugged her elbow toward the chair he pulled out. Despite the fact she'd been sitting all day, Alejandra sank into it, relishing the comfort of the padded cushion.

When he moved around the table to settle into the seat across from her, her arm felt alone without his touch. His gaze settled over her, drinking in every nuance of her features. Alejandra's hand crept to the braid that hung over her right shoulder. What must she look like after such a long, harrowing day? She probably had wispy hairs flying every direction, dirt streaking her face, and who knew what else.

Edward's lips tipped as his brown eyes darkened. He leaned forward on his elbows, shrinking the table between them. Stretching a hand, he stroked her cheek with the tips of his fingers. "You're beautiful." His voice came out deep, raspy. As if the emotion were so strong he couldn't speak it.

Their gazes locked, and she fought the urge to lean into his touch.

The dark-skinned woman appeared beside them. Edward pulled his hand back, holding her gaze for a moment longer before he turned to the woman and gave her a smile that would melt any woman's heart. But she didn't spare him a glance as she set two mugs on the table and poured steaming coffee. "Miz Myra's makin' fried chicken, and fried steak. Take yer pick."

Edward quirked a brow at Alejandra, but must have caught confusion on her face. He leaned forward and ran a finger over the top of her hand. "Miss Myra's a fine cook, so I'm sure they're both good. She makes fried steak and gravy like Anna does. It's one of my favorites." The sparkle in his eyes said it was better than good.

Alejandra's mouth curved. "I'd like to try it."

Edward turned to the woman holding the coffee pot. "Two fried steak plates, ma'am. And can you ask Miss Myra to add extra gravy, please?"

The woman bobbed her head and hurried away, and Alejandra nibbled her lower lip. "Speaking of Anna, they might be worried at the ranch. Do you think we should try to get home tonight?"

Edward leaned forward on his elbows again. "I planned to send a telegram as soon as I get you settled in the hotel. It's still another five or six hours to the ranch, so I think it'd be better to get a good night's sleep first." Twin lines appeared between his brows. "Unless you want to leave now."

Heat crept into Alejandra's chest, leaving a warm cozy feeling there. Edward was so accommodating. His exhaustion was plain from the creases at the corners of his eyes and the shadows under his lower lashes. But he still offered to ride another six hours just because she wanted to. "We can go tomorrow."

The lines between his brows softened. "Would you prefer to ride home in a buggy or on horseback?"

A buggy? The ache in her legs proclaimed how long it had been since she'd ridden a horse all day. Sitting on a leather seat would surely be easier. But then her mind brought back the memory of being snuggled behind Edward, safe in his shadow. Not much could compare to that. "I'd be happy to ride with you. Like today." Flames crept up her neck, spreading through her cheeks. How bold she was being with this man.

Edward's mouth tipped in a rakish grin that flashed his dimple, his eyes twinkling. "I was hoping you'd say that."

Footsteps sounded behind Alejandra, and the dark-skinned *camarera* appeared at their table with two plates of steaming food. A rich, comforting aroma drifted from the dishes as she studied the contents. A sizeable chunk of beefsteak and a mound of fluffy potatoes, both smothered in brown gravy like the kind Anna had taught her to make for Christmas. Some sort of a wet, green leafy food filled the remaining section of the plate. Interesting.

Edward thanked the woman, and she bobbed a curtsey before moving to another table. Alejandra looked up to see what Edward would do next. His mouth tipped on one side, and his hand stretched across the table toward her, palm up. "Shall we say a prayer?"

Tension fled from her shoulders and she reached out her own hand. His fingers hid her small hand in his strong one. "Sì." She had much to thank God for.

Edward's rich voice calmed the last of her nerves, as he thanked the Lord for the food before them. "And, Father, thank you most of all for keeping Alejandra safe. And bringing me to her…and her to me." His voice cracked on the last words, and his grip tightened around her hand.

Alejandra wanted nothing more than to snuggle in his arms, and feel his love and security wrapping around her. But the table stood between them, so she settled for squeezing his hand.

After a pause, he finished the prayer with "Gracias, Dio. Amen." When he opened his eyes, they shone with the same emotion that laced his voice during the prayer. Edward cleared his throat, then loosened his grip, rubbing the pad of his thumb over the back of her hand as he released it. "Shall we eat?"

Tearing her gaze away from Edward, she focused on the food cooling on her plate. The aroma renewed the hunger tightening her stomach. Alejandra gathered a slice of meat, potatoes, and gravy onto her fork. The moment the food touched her tongue, her senses sprang alive. Warmth spread through her mouth, as the spicy gravy blended with the hearty flavors in the meat. The beef was breaded with something rich and crunchy, adding the perfect mix of textures. Her eyelids drifted shut as the flavors collided in her mouth, then slid down her throat.

When she opened her eyes again, Edward watched her. That lone dimple pressed into his cheek as his mouth tipped in a grin. His own fork hovered over his plate.

"Good?" Both eyebrows rose to accentuate his question.

"Es increíble. You said Anna knows how to make this? I wonder if she'll teach me."

His eyes creased into a full smile. "Now that she's up and around, I'm sure she'd love to. This was one of my favorite dishes she made when we lived in South Carolina."

That sealed it. If this was Edward's favorite meal, she'd ask Anna the first possible chance when life settled down again on the ranch. And maybe there were other foods he liked that Anna could teach her.

As they ate, Alejandra's midsection ceased it's rumbling, and her eyelids grew heavy again. She forced herself to sit straight with her shoulders back, lest she fall asleep right there at the table.

"I think it's time to get you to the hotel." At Edward's deep voice, Alejandra's eyes flew open, and she jerked her chin up. Had she actually dozed? Or just let her eyes drift shut for a second. She couldn't remember.

Edward stood, tossed some paper money on the table, and eased her chair out. Inhaling a deep breath, Alejandra summoned the last of her strength to stand. He slipped her hand in the crook of his arm, and she leaned on it as he escorted her to the door.

When they stepped outside, night had fallen, bringing with it a cold breeze that slipped under her collar with icy fingers. She shivered, and Edward pulled her closer.

"We're just going next door." His voice was a husky whisper, his breath warming the side of her cheek.

When they stepped into the hotel, Alejandra was struck by the elegant décor. Even in the dim light of the lanterns mounted on walls, the rich burgundy of the curtains and rug gave the room a sophisticated air. Edward guided her to a large desk that lined one wall, behind which a tall, lean man stood, with ebony skin like the woman who'd served their food at the café. His black uniform was spotless, with gold buttons marching down the front of his coat. Buttons like those worn by the French soldiers who killed her mother.

Alejandra's hand crept to her scar before she realized it. She forced her muscles to remain still, not shrink into Edward and hide. This was a hotel clerk, not a soldier. She inhaled a shaky breath.

Chapter Twenty-Three

"OF course, Mistuh Stewart," the clerk was saying. Alejandra forced herself to focus again on the conversation between Edward and the dark-skinned man.

He fumbled with some keys hanging on nails behind the desk, mumbling something too low for them to hear. The lines on his forehead deepened, and he glanced up with his mouth pinched. "If you'll excuse me, sir. I'll be back in a minute to show you to your rooms." He disappeared through a door behind the desk.

Alejandra's eyes were drawn to the rich mahogany of the desk, with roses carved into the upper portion of each leg. The same gleaming wood lined the top of the walls where they met the ceiling, with the same roses carved on either side of the corner seams. Whomever had built and outfitted this room had cared about every detail.

She glanced at Edward, and her gaze fell into his. "It's beautiful. I've never stayed anywhere so elegant."

228

His free hand settled over hers, where she still gripped his elbow. "You deserve much finer than this." His thumb stroked the tops of her fingers. "I wish I could give you the very best."

Those chocolate eyes never left her face, but their intensity deepened. He meant those words. The very best. Somehow, just being with Edward made everything feel like the very best.

Wood scraped behind them, interrupting the moment. Edward's focus cut to something behind her, and Alejandra turned to see the lanky man stride around the desk, keys jangling in one hand and a lantern in the other.

"If you folks'll just follow me, we've got your rooms ready."

The stairs were too narrow for them to traverse side by side, so Edward ascended behind her.

"Ya'll from around Texas parts?" The man leading them turned as he spoke, the glow of the lantern illuminating portions of his face and casting others in shadows.

"Near Seguin, in Guadalupe County." Edward matched the man's conversational tone.

"Nice place, I hear. I know you said you only need the rooms one night, but we'd be happy to have you longer." They reached a landing and the man strode down a hall lined with doors on both sides. "San Marcos is a nice little town. Good people."

"I'm sure it is."

Their escort stopped at a door marked with the number three. "I think the lady will like this room." He turned the knob and pushed the door, stepping aside for her to enter.

Alejandra couldn't stop a gasp. "Es muy bonita." White lace curtains hung from a canopy bed dominating the center. The same lace draped the window, its wood frame accenting the rich walnut of the dresser and wardrobe that spanned the remaining walls.

"Please let me know if you need anythin' else, miss. I'll be happy to fetch it."

Alejandra turned to the man, keeping her focus on his face, not his uniform. In her clearest American, she said, "Thank you, sir. This looks fine."

His face spread into a wide smile, white teeth sparkling against the dark of his skin. Turning to Edward, he said, "Your room is here at the end of the hall, Mistuh Stewart."

But instead of following him, Edward eyed Alejandra. "I've asked Mister Sampson here to send a telegram to Anna and Jacob. Is there anything else you need for the night? I'm sorry you don't have a trunk or anything. If you need something, I might find a store open. Clothes to sleep in or…er, personal items." Even in the dim light she could see his face had reddened.

She stepped close enough to touch his arm, nibbling her lip against a smile. "I'm fine Edward. This is more than enough."

His gaze lifted to search hers. She released her lip and allowed the smile to bloom. "Go get some sleep."

But as he turned away, her heart pulled with him. And when she watched him trudge down the hall behind Mister Sampson, her chest squeezed with a longing she'd never experienced. *Lord, thank You for bringing me such a wonderful man to love.*

Forcing her mind away from those strong, broad shoulders, she filtered through the events of the day. When she started with a simple ride to the river, who would have thought her day would end like this?

IT was lunchtime the next day, when Edward reined Pepper off the main road and toward the farmhouse nestled in the distance. Home.

Alejandra shifted behind him, her head lifting from where her cheek had lain warm against his back. "We're home." Her voice was a groggy murmur, shooting warmth through his chest.

He'd never enjoyed a six hour ride so much as this trip home with Alejandra snuggled in behind him. He really should have rented a buggy. But they could move faster on horseback, and nothing felt so good as her arms wrapped around his waist.

"They'll be glad to see you safe." And no one could be happier than him that she was mostly un-scarred from her ordeal with those no-account snakes-in-the-grass. But he fought the urge to tighten his reins, to slow Pepper down and delay the upcoming reunion. They'd fawn over Alejandra, for sure. Probably wrap her in hugs and sweep her away into the kitchen to feed her. And maybe she needed that.

But after so much special time alone with Alejandra, it would be hard to hand her over to anyone else. A sigh escaped before he realized it.

When they rode into the ranch yard, all seemed quiet. Until a little high-pitched yap sounded from inside. Seconds later, the door burst open. Mama Sarita flew out, with Emmaline and Anna close on her heels.

He gripped Alejandra's arm as she slid off Pepper, and then she was enveloped in a flurry of hugs. As he dismounted, the women laughed and cried and embraced like they'd been separated for years.

Juan appeared at Pepper's head. He offered Edward a hand shake and an understanding grin, as his eyes flicked to the hen party in front of them. Edward wasn't sure what to say, so he just shrugged. As Juan led the horse away, Jacob strolled up with little Martin laying against his shoulder.

"Look, dear. Alejandra's finally home." Anna reached for her husband's arm, pulling him into the fray.

He nodded to Alejandra. "Awfully thankful you're back. We had a posse searching until Edward's telegraph came through. Good thing the Lord was looking out for you."

Alejandra's eyes took on a shimmer. "Yes, He was caring for me. And He used the right man to save me." Her gaze found Edward's.

He swallowed, heat crawling up his neck. What did he say in front of all these people?

Anna saved him the trouble by hooking a hand through Alejandra's arm. "Let's get you inside. I'll bet you're hungry." She shot Edward a beady-eyed look. "And that puppy's about to jump out of his skin, he's so excited to have you back. He didn't know what to do with himself with you both gone last night."

Edward trailed behind with Jacob as the women ushered Alejandra inside. When the front door opened, the puppy's high yapping bark sounded louder, although still muffled. Anna cracked the door to the parlor, and a tan fur ball darted around the edge. The little guy flung himself into Alejandra's waiting arms, and she scooped him up. She cuddled him close as he plastered her chin with puppy lick-kisses. It was hard to get a good view of her face from where he stood, but no doubt happiness shone there.

And then Alejandra turned, her eyes searching the faces for his. When she found him, her eyes lit, sparkling with a joy from within. The sea of people around her seemed to part, making way for her to come to him. As she stepped close, she held up the puppy. It was hard to pull his gaze from hers, but he finally forced himself to greet the animal with a scratch behind his ears. "Hey there, niño."

Sol answered the greeting by gnawing his hand. Sharp points dug into his skin, and Edward stifled a wince. "This boy's getting some teeth."

"I'll fill your plates while you two play with the puppy. But don't be long. I have apple pie." Something about the way Anna said "play with the puppy" caught Edward's attention.

He met her gaze in time to see a sassy quirk of her eyebrow. Then she turned with a toss of her head, and strolled down the hall to the kitchen.

"Guess I'd better get this boy to bed so he can get a decent nap." Jacob was already striding down the hall with his babe as he spoke. Although little Martin didn't seem to have any trouble sleeping perched against his father's shoulder.

"And I'll go help Anna." Mama Sarita patted Alejandra's shoulder, then turned toward the hall Anna and Jacob had just traversed. "I whipped some sweet cream earlier, so that will be good with the pie."

She paused after a few steps and looked back at them. Her eyes crinkled at the edges as she surveyed Alejandra. "I'm so glad you're home, mija." And then her gazed moved up to Edward, pinning him with intensity. "And you, son. Good job."

"Thank you." He swallowed past the lump in his throat.

Then she was gone, and he had Alejandra all to himself again. Slipping an arm around her waist, he pulled her close and pressed a kiss to her soft black hair.

She tipped her face to his, a smile touching her lips. "It's good to be home."

"Yes." His gaze dropped to those lips, so soft.

The puppy in his hand reached up and planted a lick-kiss across her chin. Alejandra jerked back, a giggle slipping from her.

Edward leaned down to let the puppy jump from his arms to the floor. "Get out of here, you rascal. That's *my* woman." He straightened to face Alejandra, not giving her a chance to react to his words. Just tightened his grip around her waist, cradled her cheek with his other hand, and brought his lips down to hers.

She was sweeter than he remembered. Her lips soft and supple, tasting of the strawberry jelly they'd eaten with biscuits on the trail. She responded to his kiss, loosening the feelings he'd held back over these two wonderful days with her. His fingers crept into her hair, pulling her closer. Closer. She wrapped her hands around his neck, and he deepened the kiss. A little moan escaped from the back of her throat, sending his heart into a frantic gallop.

A door slammed somewhere in the back of the house, barely breaking through his awareness. Nothing could stop the magic of this kiss. This woman. She pulled away, and he followed her. *Don't stop.*

She slid her hands down to his chest. "Edward." Her whisper was breathy. Half call, half reprimand.

"Alejandra." He kissed her cheek. Her jaw. She was amazing.

"Edward." That breathy call again, and she took his jaw in her hands. "They're waiting for us."

He dropped his forehead to rest on hers, soaking in deep breaths. This woman was intoxicating. He had to clear his head, although that was the last thing he wanted to do.

"LOOK how little they are."

Alejandra smiled as Emmaline wiggled her fingers through the wood slats of the chicken coop. She bent down next to the girl. "They are tiny. Just hatched this morning." A nice surprise when she'd gone to gather eggs. Definitely a better way to start the day than with her kidnapping two days before.

"Can I hold one? Please?" Emmy turned her liquid blue eyes on Alejandra first, then up to Edward who stood behind them. The setting sun framed his profile, casting shadows on his face.

He chuckled, then ambled to the door of the pen. "I guess so, if you're extra careful."

After scooping up one of the little fluff balls, he slipped back out of the coop. "Easy there, Emmy-bug." Squatting down for the girl to see, he stroked the chick with a single finger. "Just run your hand lightly like this."

As Emmaline followed his instructions, the chick "chirp, chirped" loud enough to make her jump. She snatched her hand back, then gazed up at Edward with wide eyes.

"She's talking to you. Saying 'Cheep, cheep. Hi, Emmaline. Cheep, cheep.'" His voice rose as he mimicked the bird.

Emmaline giggled, then stroked the chick, leaning close. "Hi, chicky."

After a few minutes of coddling, Edward put the fluffy animal back in the pen. "He needs to go back to his mama now." He latched the door, then turned and tweaked the end of Emmaline's nose. "And you should probably go check with your mama. She said she wanted you in the house early for bed tonight."

She scrunched her nose, shoulders slumping and arms dangling loosely. "All right."

Alejandra reached for the child. "May I have a hug, niña? Dulces sueños."

Emmaline wrapped her short arms around Alejandra, burying her face in Alejandra's red shawl. "Sweet dreams to you, too. I love you."

That now familiar ache tightened Alejandra's chest. "I love you, too." The words rasped past the emotion clogging her throat. Love for this little girl and her family had buried itself so deep in Alejandra's heart, she wouldn't ever be able to extract it.

Chapter Twenty-Four

AS Alejandra watched Emmaline trudge away, her heart was so full it ached.

Edward slipped a hand around her waist, pulling her to his side. She was tempted to lean her head on his shoulder, but he spoke before she could make up her mind.

"Care to take a short walk with me? It will be almost a full moon, and I know the spot where the stars are brightest." His voice was deep and strong in her ear.

Instead of answering with words, Alejandra turned to bestow a smile on him. She slipped out of his hold, then slid her hand into his. He entwined their fingers, her small hand fitting in his larger one as naturally as if it'd been made to rest there. With his hand covering hers, it gave her the feeling she'd never have to face anything alone again.

They walked a few minutes, skirting the outside edge of the corral fencing as dusk faded to darkness. Little sparkles of light began to illuminate the sky above. The air was chilly, a continuation of the weather Anna said was unusually warm for early March in this area. Alejandra pulled her shawl tighter against a breeze.

"Are you cold?" Edward glanced at her, his brow furrowed as he broke their companionable silence.

She sent him a reassuring smile. "No. I'm fine."

But he stopped walking and slipped his arm around her waist again, leaning back against the fence rail. "This is far enough."

Alejandra laid her head against his shoulder, staring into the twinkling sky above them, while her mind wandered. "Anna said she'd teach me to make fried steak for dinner tomorrow."

"Mmm. That sounds wonderful." His breath brushed the top of her hair as he spoke. "I'm afraid I won't be here to eat it, though. I have to go on a short trip tomorrow."

Alejandra jerked back and spun so she could see his face. Was he kidding? No, the remorse was there, clouding his features in the moonlight. A pang struck her chest, but she bit her lip against the disappointment.

"I'll be back the next day, though. And I hope to have a surprise for you."

She swallowed down the lump in her throat, forcing a light tone into her voice. "A surprise? Is it another puppy?"

A soft chuckle drifted from Edward and he pulled her into his arms. "I'm not telling."

Alejandra released a long, dramatic sigh as she rested her palms on his chest. "If you're bringing me something, I suppose

I'll wait until you come back to make the fried steak and potatoes." Or maybe she'd make them tomorrow, too, just for practice.

"That would be nice." His dark eyes twinkled in the glow of the moon. As he leaned nearer, his voice grew husky. "But anything you make is a treat."

As his lips approached hers, Alejandra's eyes drifted closed. His warm breath brushed her face, his masculine scent filling her senses. He tasted of mint and sweet buñuelo sauce, and every part of her came alive at his kiss. By the time he relinquished her mouth and held her face between his hands, Alejandra could scarcely draw breath.

But she didn't need her lungs full to know beyond a shadow of doubt, she loved this man.

ALEJANDRA released a long sigh as she sank into the kitchen chair. Across the table, baby Martin babbled at her from Mama Sarita's arms.

"I'm sure he'll be back today." Anna peered up from the needle and cloth doll in her hands. "But if you frown like that much longer, your face will freeze that way."

Alejandra's hand flew to her forehead, smoothing out the wrinkles. She should be embarrassed that her pining for

Edward was obvious. But to be honest, she was so out of sorts she couldn't bring herself to worry about the others seeing it.

Pushing to her feet again, Alejandra trudged to the stove. When she lifted the lid from the large cast iron pot, the hearty aroma of beans spread through the kitchen. It would be a poor supper if Edward came back today, but she'd cooked fried steak, mashed potatoes with gravy, and pear pie the last two nights. Of course the first night was for practice, but he said he'd be home last night. So where was he?

After stirring the beans, she let the lid drop onto the pot with a clatter. The sound didn't seem to faze baby Martin, but Sol jumped to his feet with a high puppy bark. He tilted his head at her, as if trying to decipher why she acted so strange.

He barked again, but this time looked the other way. Turning toward the front door, he continued yapping as he ran toward the hallway.

Alejandra's pulse hammered in her chest. Was someone here? Edward? She sprinted down the hall, following Sol, without taking time for another thought.

The front door opened before she could get there, and a familiar set of broad shoulders spanned the doorway. She skidded to a stop a few feet away, just before she would have thrown herself in his arms. *Slow down, Alejandra.*

Surprise raised Edward's features for a second, but it quickly morphed into pleasure. He narrowed the distance between them in two strides, wrapping his arms around her and lifting her boots off the floor with the strength of his hug.

Setting her down, he drew back just enough to see her face. "You're more beautiful than I remembered." His voice held a mixture of pleasure and awe.

"It's about time you came home."

His mouth quirked on one side, displaying that dimple that always made her heart beat double time. "Miss me?"

Her hand itched to wipe the smirk off his face. At the same time, her body threatened to pull him into a kiss that would show exactly how much she missed him.

His brown eyes darkened to a rich coffee color, and he must have read some of those thoughts on her face. "Come with me, love. Let's pack some food and have dinner by the river."

"Sì." She didn't protest as he took her hand and led her down the hall toward the kitchen.

But a twinge of fear pressed her chest. Could she go back to the river? The place of her kidnapping? With God and Edward by her side…maybe.

AS they rode, Alejandra answered Edward's questions about the last couple of days, sharing stories of baby Martin, and how many times Emmaline had begged to pet the new chicks. When she asked about his trip, the only thing he would say was, "I think it went better than I'd hoped. We'll see."

What did that mean? Since the wonder of her Texas Ranger rescue was wearing off, she'd been trying to come to terms with his doing rough Ranger work all the time. With God's help, she would do it. But accepting his career sure would be easier if Edward would open up about his trips, and share some details. That way her imagination could be somewhat confined by reality. Maybe she'd tell him that over dinner.

When the trail entered the woods that bordered the river, a knot tightened in Alejandra's stomach. The scenery looked too much like that awful day of her kidnapping.

Edward glanced over and gave her an easy smile. "Almost there."

She tried to return the smile, but had to catch her lower lip between her teeth to keep it from quivering. At last, the woods opened to the river's edge, and the trickling melody of the water seeped into her nerves, easing the tension.

While Edward tied the horses, Alejandra spread out the quilt and unwrapped the ham sandwiches she'd put together just before they left. Maybe not the most elegant meal, but eating in the fresh air with the rustling river before them might make up for the simple fare.

Edward motioned for her to sit before he did. As her blue skirt billowed around her legs, Alejandra couldn't help but feel like a princess.

He slipped his hand in hers and bowed his head. "Father, thank You for this food, and I thank You most for Your daughter who prepared it. Please bless us…and give her an open heart. In Christ's name, amen."

Alejandra's brow pinched at the last words. How could her heart be any more open than it was now? As she lifted her head and looked up at Edward, he smiled, but something about it didn't feel quite right. He looked almost...nervous.

As she pulled her hand from his to pass out the food, chilly air touched her skin, as if her hand was damp from contact with his. Now that she thought about it, his hand had been a little clammy. Was he sick? Her gaze jerked to Edward's face. He wasn't pale. If anything, more ruddy than normal.

He caught her examining him and raised a brow, his mouth tipping in that quirky smile she loved. "Everything okay?"

She placed his plate in front of him on the blanket. "I was just about to ask you the same thing. Are you feeling all right?"

"Never better." But his voice rasped, and he cleared his throat.

"I'll make you some honey tea when we get back to the ranch." She'd have to keep an eye on him to make sure it wasn't anything serious.

He chuckled, his voice back to its usual richness. "If you like."

A red bird sang from the tree branch overhead while they ate. How nice to have music with dinner. The sun hadn't set, but the light held that in-between quality of early dusk. Down river, a squirrel scampered to the water's edge and chattered at them.

Alejandra was too content with it all to finish her food, even though she'd taken half as much as she gave Edward. He hadn't finished his food either. Maybe she should have taken more time to prepare a nice dinner to go with their perfect setting.

Finally, he wrapped the remaining portion of his sandwich in the cloth, then extended a hand for her plate. "Are you done?"

She reached for it. "Yes, but I'll take care of all this."

Snatching it before she could pick up the plate, he shrugged. "It's the least I can do."

That wasn't true, especially since she was being paid to do the cleaning, but Alejandra let the comment pass.

He tucked the food and dishes in the satchel, then leaned back on one hand, and patted the blanket beside him. "Come sit with me?"

The suggestion started a flutter in her chest, and Alejandra scooted to his side, leaning back against the crook of his arm. They sat for long moments, no words needed to make the conversation perfect.

He finally broke the quiet. "You asked how my trip went." As she leaned against him, the vibrato of his voice rippled through her.

Alejandra stopped breathing for a moment, taking in his words. Edward was going to share details with her? *Thank You, Lord.*

"Sì." She tried to keep her tone neutral, not show the relief coursing through her.

He was quiet for another moment. "I resigned my commission as a Ranger."

Alejandra sucked in her breath, turning to watch his face. He kept his focus on the water, so she could only see the outline of his strong features. "I thought you liked saving people."

He faced her then, his lips curving up as he brushed a strand of hair from her cheek. "I do. That was the best part of the job." He exhaled a long breath and turned to watch the river again. "It's just...all the violence. And besides, with so much traveling, it'd be hard to settle down and take a wife."

Alejandra stilled as the words swirled in her head. A wife? Was he talking about her?

His face didn't change. He didn't look at her. And then the corner of his lip quirked, forming that dimple she loved. When his eyes darted a glance at her, his grin was undeniable. That rascal.

She raised her brows, giving him an impish look. "A wife?"

With his free hand, he reached for hers and raised it to his lips. When he met her gaze, his eyes had darkened and all humor fled his face. "Yes, my love. My beautiful, brave, kind Alejandra. Will you marry me?"

Even though she'd known what he would likely say, his words cleared every thought from her mind. Everything around them faded away as she gazed into Edward's earnest expression. Emotion welled in her chest, clogging her throat so she couldn't speak. Finally, she forced a single word through the mass.

"Sì."

Edward's face shone, like the sun breaking through the clouds. His hand slipped up to her cheek, then into her hair as he leaned close to seal the promise. His lips were strong and sure, almost possessive, yet gentle. The kiss didn't last long, but when he pulled away, every nerve in Alejandra was alive.

He searched her face, his breath coming heavier than before. "Tell me when."

A smile found its way to her mouth. "Soon."

For a long moment, she could do nothing but watch him. He was so handsome. With his earnest brown eyes, strong jaw...and that dimple. Her fingers crept up to touch it. A hint of stubble tickled her skin. He caught her palm and brought it to his lips, planting a kiss that sent tingles all the way through her.

She tried to ignore the sensation, forcing her mind to other things. "So what will you do instead of Rangering?"

"I wanted to talk to you about that." His eyes grew serious again, and he studied her. "I've been offered a job in a town not far from here. As sheriff." He slipped his hand around hers, brushing his thumb over the back of her hand. "I won't take it if it would make you uncomfortable. I could always build a house on the Double Rocking B. Jacob's offered me a share in the business. And you could be close to Mama Sarita."

As she listened to his words, love surged through Alejandra. This man was made to save people. He was talented on the ranch, yes. But God had given him a gift for helping others. And he was willing to give it up if it made her uncomfortable. *Thank you, God. You've given me more than I could have ever dreamed.*

She squeezed his hand. "I want you to be the sheriff, if that's where God calls you. Mama Sarita's in a good place at the ranch with Anna. I'll be by your side, helping people with you."

His face was a mixture of emotion. Uncertainty. Wariness. A hint of hope. "Do you mean that?"

To prove her truthfulness, she leaned forward, pulling him close for another quick kiss. As their lips parted, she met his gaze. "Every word."

Epilogue

ONE MONTH LATER

THE sun shone brightly as a light breeze ruffled the branches of the Live oak at the river's edge. Edward glanced at Jacob, who met his gaze with a single raised brow.

"She's coming, Little Brother. Don't worry."

He wasn't worried. Not really. Although he couldn't tell that by the knot in his stomach.

The small crowd milled in the open area beside the Guadalupe River. The group mostly consisted of cowpunchers from the Double Rocking B, because the women were all riding to the river with the bride.

His bride.

The knot tightened in his gut. Where was she?

A group of men gathered around Juan as he held little Martin. He was almost two months old now, and just learning

249

how to give real smiles. Amazing how a baby could make even tough cowhands go googly-eyed and talk baby-gibberish.

A horse nickered in the distance, and Edward's attention snapped toward the sound. An enclosed carriage—the new one rented from the livery in town—stopped at the edge of the tree line. Uncle Walter descended from the box in the front, and reached to assist Aunt Laura down as well.

At the edge of his vision, Edward barely realized that Reverend Walker had made his way from the crowd around Juan, to stand beside Edward. They were ready. And now he only needed his bride. Alejandra.

Curtains hung in the windows of the carriage, so he couldn't catch any glimpse of the occupants. Uncle Walter moved with painful deliberation as he stepped to the door, turned the handle, and pulled it open.

Emmaline was the first out, and after Uncle Walter helped her down the step, she sashayed across the grass. The crowd parted for her to pass through, like the little princess she was. When she reached her papa, her hand found his, and she fell into line beside him. Leaning forward, she gave Edward a beaming smile.

Next to exit the carriage was Anna, and her appearance sent a surge of pride through him. His sister hadn't looked so nice since the day she married Jacob. She and Alejandra had become like sisters these last few months. And now they really would be.

Anna moved to stand beside Aunt Laura, as Uncle Walter turned back to the coach door. Mama Sarita's head appeared, and she allowed Uncle Walter to hand her down. Her bearing was straight and regal, with the same willowy figure as Aunt Laura. Their resemblance was even more obvious when she went to stand with her sister and Anna.

Uncle Walter turned to the door one more time, and Edward's gut tightened. This had to be Alejandra. There was no one left. But after speaking to the occupant for a moment, Uncle Walter turned away, and moved to where the women stood. He extended his arm, and Mama Sarita motioned for Aunt Laura to take it.

The couple approached the wedding guests, with Anna and Mama Sarita falling into step behind them. When they neared the front of the crowd, Anna took her place across from Jacob, leaving an empty spot for Alejandra between her and the pastor. It was all like a rehearsed dance, but the waiting was enough to drive Edward mad.

"Patience, man." Jacob muttered under his breath, just loud enough for Edward to hear.

Patience. Edward inhaled deeply, then blew out the spent air. It seemed like he'd been patient for months.

And then the carriage door opened wider, and Alejandra appeared. Her magnificence stole his breath. Raven black hair framed her face, with long tendrils escaping down her back. The white lace on her gown flounced in waves down the skirt and around her collar, bringing out the rich bronze of her skin. Beautiful. Breathtaking. Amazing. Words couldn't begin to describe her. Or the effect she had in his chest.

As she approached, Alejandra floated like an angel, her gaze never wavering from his own. Her mouth tipped in a sweet smile, her eyes sparkling. His bride.

When she neared, her hand slipped into his, and Edward raised it to his lips. Reverend Walker spoke, and Edward had to force his gaze from Alejandra, as they turned to face the pastor. The clergyman began the ceremony and a feeling of awareness washed over Edward. He was standing here with Alejandra. Very soon, she would be his bride. How many times over the last months had he prayed for this moment? It wasn't until he'd fully submitted to God's will, that the Lord had brought them together. *Thank you, Father.*

When the minister spoke his name, Edward's attention snapped back to the man's words.

"Edward Thomas Stewart, wilt thou have this woman to be thy wedded wife, to live together after God's ordinance in the holy estate of matrimony? Wilt thou love her, comfort her, honor, and keep her, in sickness and in health; and, forsaking all others, keep thee only unto her, so long as ye both shall live?"

"I will." He spoke the words with the certainty that coursed through his chest.

As Alejandra made the same promise, he gave her hand a light squeeze. Did she still harbor any worries? Any regrets?

When she spoke her vows, Alejandra met his gaze, her voice strong and sure. Edward fought the urge to pull her in his arms. *Patience.* For now, he could simply enjoy the moment. The start of the rest of their lives together.

He slipped the gold band on her finger, and raised her hand to plant another kiss. Her eyes sparkled with extra moisture, and she nibbled her lower lip. An adorable habit.

At last, Reverend Walker gave him permission to kiss his bride. Time seemed to slow, as everything except Alejandra faded away. Edward fitted his left hand behind her back, and cradled her cheek with his right. She raised her face to him, her eyelids drifting closed in trusting abandon. He savored the sight, then lowered his lips to hers. Just a single, powerful kiss. But her lips sparked in him the desire for much more. Later.

As her eyes flickered open, their dark depths glazed in wonder. It was only through force of will that he didn't go back for another kiss. Alejandra blinked, as if coming back to her surroundings. Good to know the kiss affected her as much as it did him. She glanced around at their friends and family, pink stealing into her cheeks.

They were greeted with hugs and congratulations, and after a few minutes, Jacob gathered everyone to ride back to the ranch house for a post-wedding meal and celebration.

Edward snagged Alejandra's hand and led her to where he'd tied Pepper. "Are you sure you'd rather not ride in the wagon? I'm certain the ladies would make room for us both."

"I'd rather ride with you." That cute blush fanned her cheeks again, and Edward couldn't help a grin.

"Me, too." He mounted, and she pulled up behind him, wrapping both arms around his waist. A simple act of trust. He'd protect that trust with every last breath in his body.

The rest of the group mounted and started for the trail through the woods, but Edward halted his gelding at the edge of the river. Alejandra's grip tightened around him as they gazed over the water.

After a long moment she spoke. "Anna was right."

He waited for her to continue, then finally prompted. "Anna?"

"She said if I would trust God, He promised to give me a hope and a future."

Edward swallowed down a lump as she rested her head against his back.

"God kept His promise when He gave me you."

Did you enjoy this book? I hope so!

Would you take a quick minute to leave a review?
http://www.amazon.com/dp/B010EN1YSO

It doesn't have to be long. Just a sentence or two telling what you liked about the story!

About the Author

 **Misty M. Beller** writes romantic mountain stories, set in the 1800s and woven with the message of God's love.

She was raised on a farm in South Carolina, so her Southern roots run deep. Growing up, her family was close, and they continue to keep that priority today. Her husband and daughters now add another dimension to her life, keeping her both grounded and crazy.

God has placed a desire in Misty's heart to combine her love for Christian fiction and the simpler ranch life, writing historical novels that display God's abundant love through the twists and turns in the lives of her characters.

Sign up for e-mail updates when future books are available!
www.MistyMBeller.com

Don't miss the other books by

Misty M. Beller'

Mountain Dreams Series

The Lady and the Mountain Man
The Lady and the Mountain Doctor
The Lady and the Mountain Fire
The Lady and the Mountain Promise
The Lady and the Mountain Call

Texas Rancher Trilogy

The Rancher Takes a Cook
The Ranger Takes a Bride
The Rancher Takes a Cowgirl

Wyoming Mountain Tales

A Pony Express Romance
A Rocky Mountain Romance
A Sweetwater River Romance
A Mountain Christmas Romance

Heart of the Mountains

This Treacherous Journey
This Wilderness Journey
This Freedom Journey (novella)
This Courageous Journey